D1645728

CHINUA ACHEBE

Things Fall Apart

Retold by John Davey

MACMILLAN

Founding Editor: John Milne

The Macmillan Readers provide a choice of enjoyable reading materials for learners of English. The series is published at six levels – Starter, Beginner, Elementary, Pre-Intermediate, Intermediate and Upper.

Level control
Information, structure and vocabulary are controlled to suit the students' ability at each level.

The number of words at each level:

Starter	about 300 basic words
Beginner	about 600 basic words
Elementary	about 1100 basic words
Pre-Intermediate	about 1400 basic words
Intermediate	about 1600 basic words
Upper	about 2200 basic words

Vocabulary
Some difficult words and phrases in this book are important for understanding the story. Some of these words are explained in the story and some are shown in the pictures. From Pre-Intermediate level upwards, words are marked with a number like this: ...³. These words are explained in the Glossary at the end of the book.

Contents

A Note About This Story

This is a story about life in Africa before the Europeans came, and about the destruction of this life by the Europeans. The people in the story lived in a district of Nigeria called Umuofia. The people of Umuofia were farmers. They produced goods, such as palm oil, that the Europeans wanted.

Umuofia was a small district of nine villages. The people of these villages belonged to the same clan. A clan is a group of people who live together and share the same customs[1]. In time of war, all the people of the clan helped each other and fought together.

The religion of these people was not Christianity. The clansmen had many different gods. Some of the gods were very important. One of the most important gods protected the crops, and she was called the Earth Goddess. Some of the gods belonged to a man's family and wooden figures of these gods were kept in one of the family huts. The clan believed that their customs pleased the gods, and they believed their gods would punish people who broke these customs.

The people of Umuofia did not know much about the rest of the world. They grew their own food and made their own things. The clan had its own customs, religion and leaders. The way of life in Umuofia had not changed for a long time, but the people were free. They made their own decisions and they chose their own leaders. In Umuofia, a man could become a leader as a result of his own work and ability.

The People in This Story

Okonkwo   a famous man in Umuofia
Unoka   Okonkwo's father
Nwoye   Okonkwo's eldest son
Ikemefuna   a boy from another clan
Ekwefi   Okonkwo's second wife
Ojiugo   Okonkwo's third and youngest wife
Ezinma   Okonkwo's daughter
Obierika   Okonkwo's closest friend
Ezeudu   the oldest man in Umuofia
Uchendu   Okonkwo's uncle from Mbanta
Mr Kiaga   head of the church in Mbanta
Chielo   the priestess of the God, Agbala
Mr Brown   the first English missionary in Umuofia
Mr Smith   the second English missionary in Umuofia
The District Commissioner   the English administrator of the
                                  district

1
Okonkwo

Okonkwo lived in a small village called Iguedo, in the district of Umuofia. There were nine villages in Umuofia. Okonkwo was well-known by everyone in the other eight villages near his home and even by people living a long way away.

Okonkwo first became famous when he was a young man. At eighteen years old, Okonkwo fought the best wrestler[2] in all Umuofia and he won the match. He put the other man flat on his back on the floor. And everyone was proud of Okonkwo.

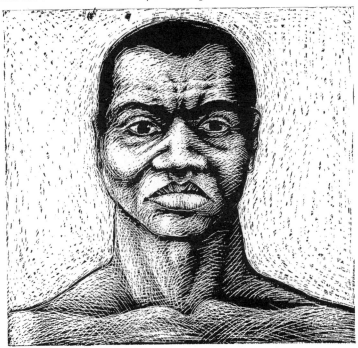

Okonkwo was now nearly forty years old. His fame had grown like a bush fire[3] and he was very famous indeed. He was tall and big and he walked like someone with springs in his feet. He had thick black eyebrows over his eyes. His nose was wide. If you did not know Okonkwo, and if you just looked at him, you would think he was a serious man and not very kind to people.

Sometimes Okonkwo would be very angry. When he was angry, Okonkwo could not say what he wanted to say. So he used his hands instead of words, and he hit people.

Okonkwo's father died ten years ago. His father was called Unoka. Unoka was a very lazy person and he did not like work. He did not like seeing blood and he was afraid of fighting. Unoka had been poor all his life because he never saved any money.

When Unoka had some money he always spent it on lots of palm wine[4]. He asked all his friends to come to his hut and drink the wine with him. They used to have a very happy time, sitting in a circle, drinking and singing songs. He was a sad-looking man and only seemed to be happy when he was making music. Music made Unoka very happy.

Okonkwo was ashamed[5] of his father. Okonkwo hated men who were lazy. And, as he was strong and brave, he hated men who were afraid of fighting in battles and wars.

When Unoka died, he left nothing for his wife and children. Okonkwo wanted to be strong and rich and powerful but he began with nothing. In the village it was not important who your father was. People knew that Okonkwo could do great things.

A few years later, Okonkwo had married three wives. He owned a large farm and he had a large compound with a thick wall of red earth round it.

Okonkwo's hut was built behind the only gate in the red walls of the compound. Each of his three wives had her own hut. Two barns were at one end of the compound, and they were full of yams[6]. At the other end of the compound there was a shed for the goats and each wife had built a small hut for some chickens near her own hut.

There was a special house near the barns. Okonkwo kept the wooden figures of his family gods in this house. It was the family shrine and Okonkwo often went there to pray for himself and his family and to give gifts to his gods.

Okonkwo had become one of the greatest men in Umuofia at that time. Everyone in his clan respected[7] him because he was not like his father.

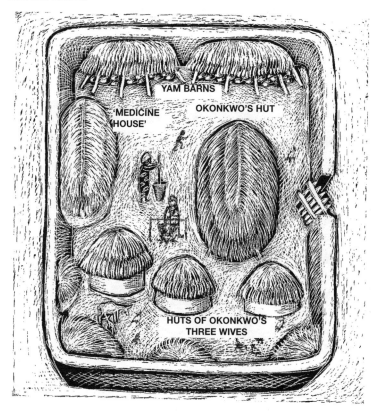

YAM BARNS

OKONKWO'S HUT

'MEDICINE HOUSE'

HUTS OF OKONKWO'S THREE WIVES

2

Ikemefuna Comes to Umuofia

The night was dark and silent. The moon was not shining and there were no happy children playing in the fields. It was quiet everywhere. The people were afraid of the dark and they kept inside their huts.

Okonkwo had gone to bed and had blown out the palm oil lamp. But just before he went to sleep the silence was suddenly broken.

Okonkwo lay in bed and heard the sound of a gong being hit by the town-crier. This man was crying out his message and hitting the gong hard.

The town-crier was asking every man in all the nine villages in Umuofia to go to the market-place in the morning. Okonkwo knew from the man's voice that something was wrong. The meeting in the market-place was going to be important. Okonkwo listened while the town-crier's voice became quieter and quieter in the distance.

Okonkwo guessed the meeting would be about a war with a neighbouring clan. But he was not afraid of this. In the last war he was the first man to bring a human head home. That was the fifth human head Okonkwo had captured. So war did not frighten him. Okonkwo would go to the meeting and find out if his guess was correct or not.

In the morning, the market-place was full of people. There were about ten thousand men waiting, and they were all talking quietly. Then one man, who was a good speaker, shouted out, 'Umuofia kwenu' which means 'We all greet you, Umuofia'. And everyone shouted back the answer 'Yaa', which means 'Umuofia thanks you for the greeting'.

The speaker shouted out four times. For the first time he faced the north; for the second, the east; then the south; and for the last time he faced the west.

There was complete silence. Everyone listened. The man who was speaking touched his white hair with his hand, and he stroked his white beard. And then he shouted, 'Umuofia kwenu' for the fifth time. And again ten thousand men shouted back 'Yaa'.

Then suddenly the man pointed his left hand towards Mbaino, which was a town not far away. As he pointed, he started speaking through closed teeth.

'The wild people of Mbaino have killed a young woman who lived here in Umuofia,' he said.

The crowd became angry, but everybody stood still. And in a calm, clear voice the speaker told the people what had happened. He told them that the wife of Ogbuefi had gone to the market at Mbaino and had been killed there by some men.

The husband of the dead woman was sitting in the crowd. He was listening and he looked sad. Everyone in the crowd felt very angry with the people of Mbaino.

After a lot of talking, the crowd at the meeting decided to send Okonkwo to Mbaino. Okonkwo would give the people of Mbaino a choice of two things. They could choose to go to war with Umuofia or they could give a young man and a young woman to the clan.

All the other districts were afraid of going to war with Umuofia, because Umuofia was very powerful and strong. If ever there was a quarrel between another district and the district of Umuofia, the other district would first try to come to a peaceful agreement.

The people of Mbaino did not want to go to war. So they sent a young man and a young woman back with Okonkwo.

Two days later, Okonkwo returned to Umuofia with a boy of fifteen and a young woman. The young woman was given to Ogbuefi, the man whose wife had been killed. Soon Ogbuefi married the young woman.

The boy, called Ikemefuna, was given to Okonkwo. Everyone agreed that Okonkwo was the best man to take care of the boy.

Okonkwo took Ikemefuna home and gave him to his first wife.

'This boy belongs to the clan. So look after him,' Okonkwo told her.

'Will he stay with us for a long time?' she asked her husband.

'Do what you are told, woman,' Okonkwo shouted.

So Okonkwo's first wife asked no more questions and took Ikemefuna to her hut.

3

Ikemefuna Finds his Best Friend

When Ikemefuna first arrived in Okonkwo's house, he was very, very frightened. He did not know where he was. He did not know why he was in Umuofia. He did not know the young woman who came with him from Mbaino, or where she had gone. And he certainly did not know that his own father had killed the woman from Umuofia.

Ikemefuna only knew that one day some men had come to his house and had talked with his father. After they had finished talking, the men had taken Ikemefuna outside and given him to a strange man. Ikemefuna's mother had cried a lot when he left, but he had not cried. He had been too surprised by what was happening.

In the first few days at Umuofia, Ikemefuna was very frightened and unhappy and lonely. Once or twice he tried to run away but he did not know where to run to. He often thought of his mother and his younger sister. And when he thought of them, he cried a lot. But Okonkwo's first wife was very kind to him and she treated Ikemefuna like one of her own children.

At first Ikemefuna was very quiet and spoke very little. When he did speak, all he said was, 'When shall I go home?' He did not eat any of the food he was given. Okonkwo was very angry when he heard that Ikemefuna would not eat. One day Okonkwo came into the hut with a big stick in his hand. He stood over Ikemefuna with the stick. Ikemefuna shook with fright. He was so frightened that he ate his yam. He did not want to be beaten by Okonkwo.

Okonkwo left the hut after Ikemefuna had eaten all his food. As soon as Okonkwo had left, Ikemefuna went outside and was sick. He was ill for three weeks and Okonkwo's first wife looked after him.

When Ikemefuna was better, he seemed to be happier and not so frightened. He was beginning to get used to his new home and he was finding some new friends. He did not cry so often and he did not think of his mother and his sister so much. In his new family, Ikemefuna found a real friend. His name was Nwoye, and he was the eldest son of Okonkwo and his first wife.

Okonkwo thought that Nwoye was very lazy and he was afraid that Nwoye would grow up to be like his grandfather, Unoka. So Okonkwo kept beating Nwoye and telling him what to do. Nwoye became a sad-looking boy. Like his mother and his sisters, Nwoye was very frightened of his father.

So when Ikemefuna arrived, Nwoye was very happy to have someone to play with him and to talk to him. Ikemefuna, too, was very pleased to find another young boy of his own age in the family. After some time, Nwoye and Ikemefuna became good friends and they were like two brothers. The two boys went everywhere together.

Nwoye was two years younger than Ikemefuna, and he followed Ikemefuna everywhere. Nwoye thought that Ikemefuna knew everything. Ikemefuna knew the names of all the birds. He could make traps to catch the little animals which came out of the forest. And he knew lots of stories which he told Nwoye.

Even Okonkwo liked Ikemefuna. But of course he did not let anyone know this. Okonkwo never let anyone see that he was kind. He always had to show people that he was strong and powerful. So Okonkwo treated Ikemefuna in the same way as he treated his other children – like a very strict father. In fact, Ikemefuna called Okonkwo 'Father'. Sometimes Okonkwo let Ikemefuna carry his stool and his goatskin bag[8] when he went to a big, important meal. This made Ikemefuna feel very proud. He felt like a real son of Okonkwo.

14

4

The Week of Peace

Every year in Umuofia the people kept a Week of Peace. This was always the week before the people planted their yams. The Week of Peace was the one week in the year when everyone had to be kind to each other. No one was allowed to fight anyone else. Husbands were not allowed to beat their wives or their children. But Okonkwo broke the peace.

One day during the Week of Peace, Okonkwo came home early in the afternoon. He sat and waited for his meal to be brought to him. His third wife, his youngest wife, called Ojiugo, was to cook that day. But Ojiugo was not at home.

That morning she had gone to see a friend and had not come back in time to cook the food. Okonkwo waited for

15

his food. It did not come, and he was feeling hungry. So he went to his wife's hut. She was not there. And the fire was cold.

'Where is Ojiugo?' Okonkwo asked his second wife.

'She has gone to see a friend,' she replied.

Okonkwo bit his lips and became angry.

Okonkwo went back to his own hut and waited for Ojiugo to come home. When she came back, he beat her very hard. He was so angry that he forgot it was the Week of Peace. Okonkwo's first two wives ran out of their huts and asked him to stop beating his youngest wife. Okonkwo's neighbours heard Ojiugo crying loudly and they came to see what was happening.

Nobody had broken the Week of Peace for many, many years. Soon everybody in the village knew that Okonkwo had beaten his wife. Before darkness came, Ezeani, the priest[9] of the Earth Goddess, came to see Okonkwo.

Okonkwo greeted Ezeani and invited him into his hut. Okonkwo offered him some kola-nuts[10] to eat.

'Take away your kola-nuts,' said Ezeani in a sharp voice. 'I shall not eat in the house of a man who does not respect our gods. I have not come on a friendly visit to see you. I have come to punish you because you have broken the Week of Peace.'

Okonkwo told Ezeani the priest that his third wife had not come home and had not cooked his dinner. He told the priest this was the reason he had beaten her. But Ezeani did not listen. Instead, he told Okonkwo to listen to him.

'Listen to me,' he said to Okonkwo. 'You are not a stranger in Umuofia. You know that we must keep a Week of Peace before we plant any crops. In that week we must live in peace with our neighbours and our family.'

Ezeani paused and looked at Okonkwo. Then he went on.

'We must not hurt anyone,' continued Ezeani, 'and we must be kind to everybody. Then the Earth Goddess will protect the crops for us and they will grow well.'

Okonkwo sat and listened and said nothing, so Ezeani continued talking.

'Okonkwo, you have done an evil[11] thing. You have beaten your wife in the Week of Peace. Your wife was not good because she stayed away from home, but you should not have beaten her.

'Your evil can hurt the whole clan,' continued Ezeani. 'The Earth Goddess may not help us and our crops may not grow well. Then we will all die of hunger.

'You must do something to please the Earth Goddess,' Ezeani said to Okonkwo. 'You must take to the shrine of the Earth Goddess one goat, one hen, a long piece of cloth, and one hundred cowrie shells[12].'

When Ezeani finished speaking, he got up and left the hut.

So the next day, Okonkwo visited the shrine of the Earth Goddess. He brought with him everything Ezeani had said.

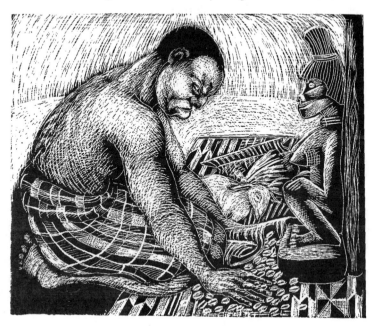

17

Okonkwo hoped the Goddess would forgive him for beating his third wife. Okonkwo was really very sorry about what he had done. He knew he had done wrong. But because he had to show everyone that he was strong, Okonkwo did not tell anyone that he was sorry.

The rest of the clan knew that Okonkwo had taken the gifts to the Earth Goddess, but they wondered if he was really sorry. They did not think Okonkwo really respected the gods of the clan. If anyone respected the gods, he would fear them and do what they told him. Okonkwo said he respected the gods, but he never showed the people that he was sorry.

In the past, men who broke the Week of Peace were often killed. They were kicked around the streets until they died. The clansmen thought that Okonkwo was very lucky to get such an easy punishment for doing such an evil thing. Okonkwo had been lucky. Now he seemed to think that he was better than the gods.

Okonkwo was a very proud man indeed.

5

The Wrestling Match

On the first day of the New Year, every family always cooked large meals and invited friends to eat with them. But the second day of the New Year was always the day for the big wrestling match. Most people did not know which of these two days they liked better. But Okonkwo's second wife, whose name was Ekwefi, liked the day of wrestling more than the day of feasting.

Ekwefi was always happy when she saw wrestling matches because she always remembered the match when she first saw Okonkwo.

Ekwefi had been a very beautiful young girl. She had fallen in love with Okonkwo as soon as she saw him at the wrestling match. She had not married Okonkwo then because he was too poor. But a few years later, Ekwefi had run away and had gone to live with Okonkwo.

All this happened many years ago. Ekwefi was now forty-five years old. But she still loved watching wrestling matches and this day she was feeling very excited.

It was nearly midday on the second day of the New Year. Ekwefi and her only daughter, Ezinma, were sitting by the fire. They were cooking the dinner.

Suddenly they heard the sound of the drums in the distance. The drums told everyone that the wrestling match would soon begin. The drumming came from the direction of the village playground. The wind brought the sound of the drums to Okonkwo's compound. The drumming was quick and happy. Okonkwo began to move his feet to the beat of the drums. Like Ekwefi, Okonkwo became very excited. Okonkwo and his family walked to the playground. Nearly everybody in the village was there – the men, the women and the children. All the people stood round in a circle. The centre of the playground was empty. The old men and the important men in the village sat on stools brought by their own children. Okonkwo sat on the stool Ikemefuna had carried for him. Everybody else was standing up.

The wrestlers were not at the playground yet and everyone was listening to the drummers. There were three drummers and they sat in front of the circle of people who were watching. The three men had seven drums in a long wooden basket. They were beating the drums with sticks, moving from one drum to another one very quickly.

At last, the two teams of wrestlers danced into the circle. The crowd shouted as loud as they could and they clapped their hands hard together. The noise of the drums got louder and the people pushed forward. They wanted to see everything.

The wrestling match started with boys who were fifteen or sixteen years old. There were only three boys in each team. They were not good wrestlers. The first two matches were finished very quickly. But the third match made everyone shout with great joy.

One of the boys moved very quickly. He moved so quickly that nobody had time to see what was happening. Almost immediately the other boy was flat on his back on the ground. The crowd jumped up and down and shouted and clapped. They made so much noise that no one could hear the drummers beating their drums.

Okonkwo was so excited that he jumped to his feet and sat down again. Three young boys ran towards the boy who had won. His name was Maduka and he was the son of Obierika, Okonkwo's friend. The three boys picked Maduka up and carried him on their shoulders through the cheering crowd.

Then the drummers stopped and had a short rest. They wanted a rest before the start of the important matches. Their bodies shone with sweat. They were very hot indeed.

When the drummers had rested and were ready again, they picked up their sticks and began to drum loudly. It was the time for the men to wrestle now. The two teams stood facing each other across the empty circle. Then one young man from one team danced across the centre of the circle to the other side. He pointed to one person in the other team who he wanted to fight. Then they both danced back to the centre and came close together to start wrestling.

There were twelve men on each side and each side took it in turns to ask another person to fight. The last match was between the two leaders of the two teams. These two men were the two best wrestlers in all the nine villages in Umuofia. Everyone in the crowd wondered which man would win.

When this last match began it was getting dark. The sun had gone down. The drummers beat their drums wildly and the crowd shouted and cheered as loud as they could. Everyone was

The third match made everyone shout with joy.

so excited that they pushed nearer the centre of the circle and nobody could keep them back.

The crowd knew these two wrestlers. They had seen these two men fight in a wrestling match the year before. In that match they were equal and neither of the men was thrown on the ground. Everyone wondered if the same thing would happen again.

One of the wrestlers, called Ikezue, held out his right hand. The other man, called Okafa, grabbed Ikezue's hand and they came close together. It was an exciting match. Ikezue tried to put his right heel behind Okafa to push him over backwards. But Okafa was waiting for this. The two men held each other tightly. The muscles in their arms and on their backs stood out. The fight looked equal again.

At that moment, Ikezue bent down quickly on one knee. He tried to throw Okafa backwards over his head. But this was a wrong thing to do. It was a bad mistake. Okafa suddenly raised his right leg and he put it over Ikezue's head. Then he pushed Ikezue down on to the ground with all his strength. Ikezue fell flat on his back.

Okafa was the winner. The crowd cheered loudly and the people who had wanted Okafa to win ran towards him. They picked Okafa up and put him on their shoulders and carried him home. On the way to their village they sang happily and the young girls clapped their hands. Everyone was very pleased and they were proud of Okafa. The New Year had begun happily for them all.

6

Ikemefuna is to Go Home

Ikemefuna lived with Okonkwo and his family for three years, and the leaders of the clan seemed to have forgotten about him.

Ikemefuna was now a young man of eighteen and he was tall and strong and very lively. He was very happy living with Okonkwo's family and he was like a real elder brother to Nwoye. Ikemefuna and Nwoye were great friends and they spent most of the time with each other. Nwoye felt grown up when he was with Ikemefuna.

Both Ikemefuna and Nwoye sat with Okonkwo in his own hut. They thought they were too old to sit with Nwoye's mother and sister. Sometimes Nwoye's mother asked Nwoye to find wood for her or to do some other job. When his mother wanted Nwoye, Nwoye would pretend to be angry. He would complain about women and the trouble they made for men.

Okonkwo was very pleased with Nwoye as he seemed to be becoming a strong young man. Okonkwo knew that Ikemefuna had helped change Nwoye from a weak boy into a strong young man.

Okonkwo was very proud of both boys. He wanted Nwoye to be a strong man. He wanted him to be a man who could look after Okonkwo's family when Okonkwo was dead. Okonkwo wanted Nwoye to be rich, with enough food to feed his own family. So he was very happy to hear Nwoye complain about women. This showed that when Nwoye was older he would be able to control his family, and especially his wives.

Okonkwo often asked the two boys to sit with him in his hut and he told them stories about Umuofia. These stories were true and they were about fighting and war. Nwoye listened to the stories and knew that he ought to like them. But secretly he still liked the stories his mother used to tell him when he was young.

His mother's stories were not about fighting and wars but about animals and birds. Nwoye knew these stories were for stupid women and children and he knew that his father wanted him to be a man. So Nwoye pretended to like the stories his father told him. Then Okonkwo was happy and he did not beat Nwoye any more.

One day, Okonkwo was sitting in his hut with Ikemefuna and Nwoye. He was eating some food and drinking palm wine. Suddenly his friend, Ogbuefi Ezeudu, came into the hut.

Ezeudu was the oldest man in that part of Umuofia. He was a very brave man and everyone respected him. Okonkwo offered Ezeudu some food, but he would not take any. Ezeudu asked Okonkwo to go outside the hut as he wanted to tell him something. The two men walked outside so the two boys could not hear them talking. Ezeudu spoke.

'That boy, Ikemefuna, calls you "Father". Do not help to kill him,' said Ezeudu to Okonkwo.

Okonkwo was very surprised to hear these words. He was going to speak, when Ezeudu spoke again.

'Yes,' said Ezeudu, 'Umuofia has decided to kill Ikemefuna. Our clan god, the Oracle[13] of the Hills and the Caves, has said he must be killed. The people will take Ikemefuna outside Umuofia and they will kill him there.'

Okonkwo did not speak, so Ezeudu continued.

'But you must not help kill Ikemefuna,' said Ezeudu. 'He calls you "Father" and you must not help to kill him. If you help kill him the Oracle will not be pleased.'

Early the next day, a group of important men from all the nine villages in Umuofia went to Okonkwo's house. They sent Ikemefuna and Nwoye out of the hut. Then they spoke quietly to Okonkwo. These men stayed for only a short time. Then they left. Okonkwo sat in his hut with his head resting in his hands. He did not move.

In the afternoon, Okonkwo called Ikemefuna into his hut.

Okonkwo told him that the men were going to take him home the next day. Nwoye cried when he heard that Ikemefuna was going away. Okonkwo immediately beat Nwoye very hard because he was crying.

Ikemefuna did not know what to think. He did not really want to go home. He had forgotten what his home was like. Of course, he still missed his mother and his sister. Ikemefuna wanted to see them again. But he felt a little afraid. Ikemefuna felt he was not going to see either his mother or his sister ever again.

7

The Death of Ikemefuna

The next day, the men returned to Okonkwo's house. They had a big pot of wine with them. They wore their best clothes. They looked as if they were going to a big meeting of the clan or on a visit to another village. These men had bags over their shoulders and they carried matchets[14]. Okonkwo got ready quickly. They all left the compound and Ikemefuna carried the pot of wine on his head.

At first all the men were talking and laughing. But the further they went, the quieter they became. The sun got hotter and the birds in the forest began to sing. The only noise was the birds singing and the sound of men's footsteps on the ground. Everybody was silent. Ikemefuna wondered why nobody was talking and he felt a little afraid.

The footpath got very narrow. They were right in the middle of the forest. The trees were getting bigger and taller. Some were covered with climbing plants. The forest looked as if nobody

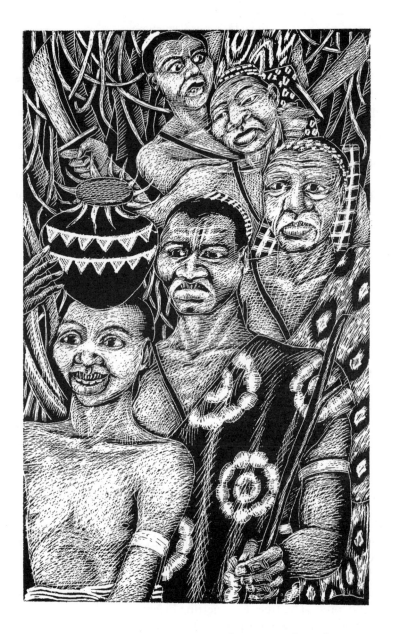

The footpath got very narrow. They were right in the middle of the forest.

had been in it for years and years. The sun shone through the leaves and the trees and made patterns of light and shade on the ground.

Ikemefuna heard a man whispering behind him. He turned round to see who it was. The man was telling the people to hurry up.

'We still have a long way to go,' the man said, 'so we must hurry.'

Then this man and another one went to the front and started walking more quickly. Everyone then walked more quickly. Ikemefuna was in the middle of them all. The men were still carrying their matchets and Ikemefuna still had the pot of wine on his head.

At first, Ikemefuna had been frightened. But he was not frightened any more because Okonkwo was walking right behind him. Ikemefuna felt safe. Okonkwo was like a real father to him. Ikemefuna had never liked his own father and he had forgotten him after three years. But he loved Okonkwo.

Suddenly one of the men walking behind Ikemefuna made a noise in his throat. Ikemefuna looked round and the man told him to walk on and not to look back. He spoke in a frightening voice. His voice made Ikemefuna's whole body go very cold. Ikemefuna became frightened. His hands shook a little as they held the pot of wine.

Ikemefuna looked back again quickly. Okonkwo was not walking behind him now. He was right at the back of the line of men.

Ikemefuna's legs began to shake. He was afraid to look back again. The man behind him raised his matchet quietly and quickly and brought it down on Ikemefuna's head. Okonkwo heard the matchet hit the pot of wine. The pot fell off Ikemefuna's head and broke on the ground. Okonkwo heard Ikemefuna cry out.

'My father, they have killed me,' Ikemefuna cried.

Ikemefuna ran towards Okonkwo. Okonkwo was very afraid,

but he raised his own matchet and brought it down onto Ikemefuna's head and killed him. Okonkwo did not want to do this. He was very afraid. And he loved Ikemefuna. But he was afraid that his friends would think he was weak if he did not kill Ikemefuna.

The Oracle had said that Ikemefuna had to die. But it had also said that Okonkwo should not help to kill Ikemefuna. Okonkwo had broken one of the rules of the clan because he was so proud.

As soon as Okonkwo walked into the house that night, Nwoye felt and knew that Ikemefuna had been killed. Something deep down inside him seemed to break. It was like the breaking of a tight string. Nwoye did not cry, but his whole body went weak.

He had once felt the same way when he had been much younger. One day he had been walking through the forest with his family. It was night and in the darkness they had heard the sound of a baby crying. The women had stopped talking and they walked quickly.

Nwoye had heard stories that twin[15] babies brought bad luck to their parents. So mothers who had twins put the twins into pots and threw them away into the Evil Forest[16]. That was the first time Nwoye had seen this done. He felt cold all over when he heard the baby crying and he felt frightened too. It was the feeling you have when you walk alone in the forest at night when it is very dark.

Nwoye had the same weak feeling now when Okonkwo walked into the house without Ikemefuna. At that moment, Nwoye lost his love for his father. Nwoye felt very unhappy and he felt very, very lonely. His life was now empty. Now he had nobody to talk to.

8

Okonkwo Talks to a Friend

Okonkwo did not eat any food for three days after the death of Ikemefuna. But he drank palm wine from early in the morning until late at night. He was very tired and his eyes were red and angry looking. Okonkwo often called Nwoye into his hut. He wanted Nwoye to sit with him. But Nwoye was afraid and used to leave the hut quietly if his father went to sleep.

Okonkwo did not sleep at night time. He tried not to think about Ikemefuna, but he couldn't stop thinking about him.

One night he couldn't sleep at all so he got up from his bed and walked around the compound. His legs were very weak and Okonkwo found it difficult to walk.

He felt very cold and his body shivered[17].

On the third day after Ikemefuna's death, Okonkwo asked his second wife, Ekwefi, to cook some bananas for him. Ekwefi was a good cook and she cooked bananas with fish. This was the way Okonkwo liked them. When the food was ready, Ezinma, Okonkwo's daughter, took it to him.

'You have not eaten any food for two days,' Ezinma said. 'You must eat all this.'

Ezinma sat down on the ground near Okonkwo, and put her legs straight out in front of her. Okonkwo ate the food quickly. He did not enjoy it. He looked at Ezinma who was ten years old.

I wish Ezinma was a boy, Okonkwo said to himself. And he gave her a piece of his fish.

'Go and bring me some cold water to drink,' Okonkwo told her.

Ezinma ran out of the hut eating the piece of fish, and came back with a bowl of cool water. Okonkwo took the bowl and drank the water quickly. He ate some more fish and then pushed the plate away from him. Ezinma took the plate and the bowl and went back to her mother's hut.

I wish Ezinma were a boy, Okonkwo said to himself again.

Okonkwo then thought about Ikemefuna again and he shivered. He tried to forget Ikemefuna but he could not do so. He thought about him all the time.

Why have I become like a shivering old woman? Okonkwo asked himself. Everybody in all the nine villages knows that I am a brave man. I have killed five men in battle. Why am I like a weak woman because I have also killed a young boy? I have become like a woman.

Thinking these thoughts, Okonkwo jumped to his feet and went to visit his friend, Obierika. Obierika was sitting under a tree, in the shade. The two men greeted each other and Obierika took Okonkwo into his hut.

'I was coming to see you soon,' Obierika said to him.

'Is everything all right?' asked Okonkwo.

'Yes. I am happy because my daughter is going to get married soon,' replied Obierika.

Just then, Obierika's son, Maduka, came into the hut. Maduka greeted Okonkwo and turned to leave. Okonkwo called out to him.

'Come and shake hands with me,' Okonkwo said. 'I saw you wrestling three years ago, when you threw the other boy onto the ground. You made me very happy.'

Maduka smiled and shook hands with Okonkwo. Then he left the hut. After he had gone, Okonkwo turned to Obierika.

'Maduka will be very successful in life,' said Okonkwo. 'If I had a son like him, I would be very happy.

'I am worried about Nwoye,' continued Okonkwo. 'If he wrestled with a bowl of yams, the bowl of yams would throw him on the ground. None of my sons is like me. Who will take my place when I am dead?

'If Ezinma were a boy I would be very happy indeed. Ezinma's ideas about life are good,' said Okonkwo.

'Don't worry about your sons,' replied Obierika. 'They are still very young.'

'Nwoye is now fifteen,' said Okonkwo. 'When I was his age, I was looking after myself. No, my friend, Nwoye is not too young. He will not change. I have done my best to make him grow into a man, but he is too much like his mother.'

Obierika thought, Nwoye is too much like his grandfather, Unoka. But he did not say this to Okonkwo. Instead, he spoke to Okonkwo about the killing of Ikemefuna.

'I don't understand why you refused to come with us to kill that boy, Ikemefuna,' Okonkwo said to Obierika.

'Because I didn't want to,' replied Obierika angrily. 'I was too busy.'

'Don't you think that the Oracle was right when it said that Ikemefuna had to die?' asked Okonkwo.

'I think the Oracle was right,' said Obierika. 'But the Oracle did not ask me to help kill Ikemefuna.'

'No. Maybe not,' replied Okonkwo. 'But someone had to kill him. If everyone was afraid of blood, no one would have killed the boy.'

These words made Obierika very angry. He thought that Okonkwo was calling him a coward.

'You know, Okonkwo,' said Obierika, 'that I am not afraid of blood. And let me tell you one thing, my friend. If I were you, I would have stayed at home. I would not have killed Ikemefuna. What you have done will not please the Earth Goddess. She said that Ikemefuna had to be killed, but she told you not to help kill him.'

'The Earth Goddess cannot punish me,' replied Okonkwo. 'I did not want to kill Ikemefuna. The Oracle said Ikemefuna must die.'

'That is true,' continued Obierika. 'If the Oracle said that my son must die, I would not disagree with the Oracle. But I would not kill him myself.'

And so the two men talked about the killing of Ikemefuna for a long time.

Okonkwo felt better after he had talked to Obierika about the murder. Okonkwo had been silly. He had done too much thinking and not enough work. But now he felt happier.

'I must go home and do some work on the farm,' Okonkwo said. 'I must tap my palm trees and see how they are.'

'Well, goodbye,' said Obierika. 'Come back and see me soon.'

'I shall return very soon as I want to see your brave son, Maduka, again,' replied Okonkwo.

Then Okonkwo left and went back to his own hut. He felt a much happier person.

9

Ezinma's Illness

For the first time in three months, Okonkwo slept well. He was woken up very early in the morning. Somebody was knocking hard on his door.

'Who is that?' he shouted. It was Ekwefi.

'Ezinma is dying,' she said in a very sad voice.

Okonkwo jumped out of bed quickly, opened the door and ran to Ekwefi's hut. Ezinma was lying on a mat near a big fire. The fire had been burning all night. But although Ezinma was near the fire, she was shivering.

'Ezinma has a fever[18],' Okonkwo said.

Then Okonkwo picked up his matchet and went into the forest to cut some leaves and some grasses. With the leaves and grasses he could make medicine to stop the fever.

Ekwefi knelt down beside Ezinma. She felt the child's head. It was hot. Ekwefi had only one child and she loved Ezinma very much. Ekwefi had had ten children and nine had died when they were still very young. So Ekwefi loved Ezinma very much indeed.

When Ezinma was born she was a weak baby. But everyone thought she would live. So Ekwefi looked after her very carefully so that she would become a strong girl. Sometimes Ezinma would be lively and very healthy. At other times she would be tired and ill.

Everyone knew that Ezinma was an *ogbanje*. An *ogbanje* is a child that dies many times and returns to its mother to be born again. An *ogbanje* child is often healthy one day and ill the next.

Ezinma was like this. But Ezinma had lived longer than most *ogbanje* children. Perhaps she had decided to stay alive. Ekwefi began to believe that Ezinma would not die.

An *ogbanje* child is joined to the world of the Spirits[19] by a special kind of stone. If this special stone can be found and can be destroyed, then the child will live.

A medicine man[20] had found Ezinma's stone when she was nine years old. It was a smooth stone, wrapped in a dirty piece of cloth. That medicine man was famous in all Umuofia. He knew everything about *ogbanje* children and where the special stones could be dug up. He had found Ezinma's special stone, and he had dug it up and destroyed it. So Ezinma was not joined to the world of Spirits any more. Ekwefi had believed that Ezinma could not die. But now Ekwefi was very frightened. Ezinma was very ill. Perhaps she *would* die from her fever.

Okonkwo returned from the forest, carrying a large bundle of leaves and grasses and roots of trees. These would make good medicine. He went into Ekwefi's hut.

'Give me a pot,' Okonkwo said to his wife. 'And leave the child alone.'

Okonkwo chose the best leaves and grasses and roots and cut them up. He put them into the pot. Ekwefi poured some hot water onto them. She then put the pot on the fire. Okonkwo left her and went to his own hut.

'Watch the pot carefully,' he told Ekwefi as he was leaving. 'Don't let it boil over. If it does, all the goodness in the leaves and roots will go.'

So Ekwefi watched the pot very carefully. It did not boil over. Later, Okonkwo came back to look at the pot. It was ready.

'Bring a small stool and a thick mat,' Okonkwo told Ekwefi.

Okonkwo took the pot and put it on the floor by the stool. He then carefully picked up Ezinma and put her on the stool near the steaming pot.

Okonkwo threw the thick mat over the top of both Ezinma

and the pot. Ezinma tried to get away from the hot, thick steam, but Okonkwo held her down. She started to cry.

At last the mat was taken away. Ezinma was very wet and very hot. Ekwefi dried her with a cloth. Then she picked Ezinma up and put her on a dry mat on the floor. Ezinma was soon fast asleep.

After a few days, Ezinma was better and was walking about. Ekwefi was very happy. She knew that Ezinma was not going to die now.

10

Ezinma Goes Away

The night was very, very dark. There was no moon. Ezinma and her mother, Ekwefi, had finished eating their supper. They were sitting on a mat on the floor, near a lamp. They could not see anything without the lamp. It was too dark to do any work so Ekwefi and Ezinma told stories to each other.

Ezinma was telling a story when she suddenly stopped. She stopped because she heard a loud high voice shouting in the distance. It was the voice of Chielo, the priestess of the god Agbala.

Chielo was prophesying. She often prophesied about people. She told people what was going to happen to them. But tonight her words were meant for Okonkwo. So everyone in Okonkwo's family listened carefully.

'Agbala do-O-oo! Agbala do-O-oo,' said the voice. 'Okonkwo! Agbal eken gio-o-o-o! Agbala cholu ifu ada ya Ezinmao-o-o-o!'

These words meant that the god, Agbala, wanted to see Ezinma.

Okonkwo went outside the hut. Chielo, the priestess, went into Okonkwo's compound and talked to him.

Chielo told Okonkwo many times that the god, Agbala, wanted to see Ezinma. Okonkwo replied every time that Ezinma was asleep and he asked Chielo to come back for Ezinma the next morning. Chielo took no notice of Okonkwo and still asked for Ezinma. Okonkwo still asked the priestess to come back the next morning because Ezinma had been ill and was fast asleep.

Suddenly Chielo screamed out loudly.

'Take care, Okonkwo,' she said. 'Do not ignore the wishes of Agbala. Is it wise for a man to ignore the wishes of a god? Take care.'

Usually everyone obeyed Chielo immediately. They did not ask questions. But Okonkwo wanted to make Chielo wait for Ezinma. He was not really afraid of Agbala.

Chielo walked straight past Okonkwo and went into Ekwefi's hut.

'Where is Ezinma?' she asked. 'Agbala wants to see her.'

'Where does Agbala want to see Ezinma?' asked Ekwefi.

'In his house in the hills and the caves,' replied Chielo.

'I will come with you,' said Ekwefi.

'How dare you go to see Agbala unless he asks to see you!' said the priestess. 'Give me Ezinma.'

Ekwefi gave Ezinma to Chielo.

'Come, my dear,' said Chielo to Ezinma. 'I will carry you on my back. Then you will not know that the journey is long.'

Ezinma began to cry because she was afraid.

'Don't cry,' said Ekwefi. 'The priestess will bring you back home soon.

'Don't be afraid,' said Ekwefi again; and she stroked Ezinma's head.

Then Chielo, the priestess, went down on one knee and Ezinma climbed onto her back. Ezinma was still crying a little.

'Agbala do-o-o! Agbala ekeneo-o-o-o!' Chielo shouted these

greetings again to her god as she left the hut. Ezinma cried loudly and called to her mother. The two voices of Ezinma and Chielo disappeared into the thick darkness of the night.

Ekwefi suddenly felt very weak. She looked in the direction of the voices. Soon Ekwefi could not hear Ezinma's voice. She heard only the voice of Chielo, which was getting quieter and quieter in the distance.

'Why are you standing there looking stupid?' said Okonkwo to his wife. 'Ezinma hasn't been stolen from you.'

But Ekwefi did not listen to her husband. She stood still for a short time and then she walked quietly through Okonkwo's hut and went outside.

'Where are you going?' asked Okonkwo.

'I am going to follow Chielo,' replied Ekwefi. And she walked out into the darkness. Okonkwo sat down and thought.

11

The Cave of Agbala

The voice of the priestess was getting quieter and quieter. Ekwefi hurried to the footpath outside the compound and turned left to follow the voice.

It was a very dark night and Ekwefi could not see anything. She began to run and she fell down many times. The night was cold but Ekwefi was hot because she was running.

The priestess was still shouting out in the darkness ahead. Ekwefi followed Chielo. She did not want to get too close to Chielo. If Chielo turned round suddenly and saw Ekwefi, she would be very, very angry. But Ekwefi did not walk very far behind Chielo because she did not want to lose the priestess.

Suddenly Ezinma sneezed and Ekwefi became happier. She knew that Ezinma was still alive. And then the priestess suddenly screamed out.

'Somebody is walking behind me!' shouted the priestess. 'Go back whoever you are. Agbala will punish you. He will twist your neck until your head is looking backwards.'

When Ekwefi heard these words she stood still. She was terrified. She did not know if she ought to go on or to return home. She waited until the priestess was further ahead and then she began to follow her again.

At last, Chielo reached the path to the caves.

The priestess walked on and went into the entrance of one of the caves. This was the home of the god, Agbala.

The entrance to the cave was very small and Ekwefi did not know how the priestess and Ezinma got through it. Ekwefi stood outside the cave and started to cry. Tears ran down her face. She sat down on a large stone and waited. She was not afraid now because she was sure Ezinma would be all right.

Ekwefi sat and waited for a long time. Suddenly she heard a noise behind her. She turned round and saw a man standing there. He had a matchet in his hand. Ekwefi screamed and jumped to her feet.

'Don't be foolish,' said the man's voice.

It was the voice of Okonkwo. He had followed Ekwefi.

'I thought you were going into the cave after the priestess,' he said. 'You would be foolish to do that.'

Ekwefi did not answer her husband. But she was very pleased to see him. She cried with happiness. Ekwefi knew also that Ezinma was safe.

'Ekwefi, go home and sleep,' said Okonkwo. 'I will wait here.'

'I will wait here with you,' said Ekwefi. 'It is almost dawn. The first cock has just crowed.'

So Okonkwo and Ekwefi sat outside the cave and waited.

A few hours later, Chielo, the priestess, crawled out of the cave on her stomach. She crawled out like a snake. Ezinma was still on Chielo's back. Chielo looked straight ahead and walked back to Okonkwo's village. Ekwefi and Okonkwo walked behind her, at a distance.

Chielo walked into Okonkwo's compound and into Ekwefi's hut. She went into Ekwefi's bedroom and put Ezinma carefully on a bed. Then the priestess walked away and said nothing. She did not speak to anybody.

Ezinma was safely back at home. She was alive and well. Both Ekwefi and Okonkwo were very happy. They knew Ezinma would not die now.

12

The Funeral of Ezeudu

Go-di-di-go-di-go. Di-go-go-di-go. This was the sound made by the big drum being beaten.

Diim! Diim! went the big gun as well.

It was early in the morning. It was dark and everyone was still in bed and fast asleep. But the sound of the drum and the gun woke everybody up. The men in the villages listened carefully. They were worried because the drum meant that somebody was dead.

The sound of the drum went a long way. The way the drum was beaten gave a message. This drum told everyone in all the nine villages that somebody had died. The drum beat out the news and said, 'Umuofia obodo dike', which means "the land of the brave". 'Umuofia obodo dike' it said, many times.

Everyone in the villages listened to the drum and was afraid. They did not know who was dead.

Then the drum beat the name of the village where the dead man lived. It was Okonkwo's village. At last, the drummer beat out the name of the dead man. His name was Ezeudu. As Okonkwo heard the name of his friend, Ezeudu, he shivered. Okonkwo remembered the last time the old man had come to see him. It was the time when Ezeudu had said to Okonkwo, 'That boy, Ikemefuna, calls you Father. Do not help to kill him.'

Ezeudu was a very important man in the village and so everyone in the clan was at this funeral. Drummers were beating the drums of death, and the guns were firing to show him respect. Men ran about in all directions. They cut down every tree they could see and killed every animal they found. They jumped over walls and danced on the roofs. As Ezeudu was an important man, he was going to be buried after dark. A torch of fire was going to be the only light at the funeral.

Just before Ezeudu was buried, the drummers beat louder and the men jumped up and down into the air. Some people were firing guns. Okonkwo had brought an old gun with him and he was waving it high in the air. The drums beat and the men danced. They all became very excited. Guns fired the last shots before Ezeudu was buried. The noise was very great.

Then suddenly, a cry of pain and shouts of fear came from the centre of all the noise. Everyone became silent immediately. A young boy lay dead in the centre of the crowd. He lay in a pool of blood. The young boy was one of the sons of the dead man, Ezeudu. He was only sixteen years old.

The young boy had been dancing with his brothers in the last dance for his father. Okonkwo's gun had exploded[21] by accident and a piece of iron from the gun had gone into the boy's heart and killed him.

Nobody knew what to do. Everybody ran about in all directions. Everybody was afraid. All the clan had seen a lot of death and murder in Umuofia. But this killing was the most terrible thing that had ever happened.

As soon as Okonkwo knew that he had killed the boy, he knew what he had to do. He had to leave Umuofia and leave the clan. Okonkwo had committed a crime[22] against the Earth Goddess because he had killed another person in the clan.

There were two kinds of crime against the Earth Goddess. One was called a male crime. This was when the crime was not an accident. The other was a female crime. This was when the crime was an accident. Okonkwo had killed the boy accidentally. As this was a female crime, Okonkwo would have to leave his own clan for seven years and go away. After seven years he could return.

So that night, Okonkwo packed up his most valuable things. His wives and children cried a lot because they were very unhappy. They did not want to leave Umuofia. Okonkwo's

A young boy lay dead in the centre of the crowd.

friends came and carried all Okonkwo's yams to Obierika's barn. Obierika was going to look after the yams while Okonkwo was away.

Before daylight came, Okonkwo and his family left his village in Umuofia. They were going to his mother's village, a long way away. His mother's village was called Mbanta.

After the sun came up, many of Ezeudu's friends came to Okonkwo's compound. They wore special war clothes. These men set fire to Okonkwo's huts. They knocked down the red wall. They killed all his animals and they knocked down his barn. They destroyed everything that Okonkwo owned.

The men were punishing Okonkwo for killing Ezeudu's son. The Earth Goddess had told them to destroy everything in Okonkwo's compound. These men still liked Okonkwo. They were only cleaning the land which Okonkwo had made dirty with the blood of a young boy in the clan.

Obierika, Okonkwo's friend, was one of the men who destroyed Okonkwo's compound. After the men had destroyed everything, Obierika sat down and thought about his friend. Obierika was sad. He asked himself why any man had to leave his own home because he had killed somebody by accident. But Okonkwo had committed a crime against the clan and the Earth Goddess had to punish him.

13

Okonkwo Arrives in Mbanta

Okonkwo reached Mbanta safely with his three wives and eleven children. When he got there all his mother's family were pleased to see him. Okonkwo was met by his uncle, Uchendu. Uchendu was one of the oldest men in the family and he told Okonkwo that he was welcome to stay in Mbanta.

As soon as Uchendu met Okonkwo, he saw that Okonkwo was unhappy. Uchendu guessed that Okonkwo and his family had been sent away from Umuofia and he did not ask any questions.

The next day, Okonkwo told Uchendu that he had accidentally killed a boy at Ezeudu's funeral. Okonkwo had to leave Umuofia for seven years.

Okonkwo's uncle listened to the story and he said nothing until Okonkwo had finished.

Then Uchendu spoke.

'Your crime is not too serious since it is a female crime,' said Uchendu. 'So you must not be too sad.'

Uchendu gave Okonkwo a piece of ground where he could build a new compound. Okonkwo was also given two or three pieces of land to grow crops on. Okonkwo built a hut for himself and three huts for his wives. Then he put a wooden figure of his own god in his hut.

Uchendu had five sons. Each son gave Okonkwo three hundred yam seeds to plant on the land. It was nearly time for the rain to come, so Okonkwo was ready to plant the yam seeds.

At last the rain came. It came very suddenly and it was very heavy. Before the rain started all the grass was brown and burnt. The ground felt like burning coal when you walked on it with your bare feet. Then suddenly the thunder came. It was noisy and sounded like sheets of metal being banged together.

A very strong wind blew and the palm trees moved backwards and forwards. When the rain started it came like small pieces of ice. These pieces hurt your body when they hit you. The young boys and girls ran about happily. They picked up the pieces of ice and put them in their mouths. The ice melted in their mouths and made the children feel cool.

The birds began to sing and the trees and plants woke up again. It had not rained for many months. Everyone was happy and pleased that the rain had come at last. It was time to plant the yam seeds once more.

Okonkwo and his family worked very hard. But Okonkwo was not a young man any more. When he was young he had liked his work very much, but now he did not. He did not think that work was a pleasure any more. When he was not working, he sat in silence and was half asleep.

All his life, Okonkwo had one very big wish. He wanted to become one of the leaders of his own clan. He had had this wish since he was a young man. He still wanted this more than anything else, but now this wish was not possible. Okonkwo would never be a leader of his clan. He had been sent away from Umuofia. When he returned to Umuofia after seven years, he would never be chosen as a leader.

Uchendu saw that Okonkwo was unhappy and miserable so he decided to talk to Okonkwo about his life. He wanted to make Okonkwo happier.

So one day Uchendu called together his sons, his daughters and Okonkwo. The men sat on mats on the floor and the women sat on mats made of grass. Uchendu pulled his beard gently. Then he began to speak. He spoke quietly and slowly and he chose his words carefully.

'I want really to speak to Okonkwo,' Uchendu said. 'But I want all of you to listen to me. I am an old man and you are all young. I know more about the world than any of you. If you think that you know more than me, then say so now.'

Uchendu stopped talking and waited. Nobody spoke, so Uchendu continued.

'Why is Okonkwo here today with us?' Uchendu asked. 'Our clan is not his clan. We are only his mother's relations. Okonkwo doesn't belong here. He has been sent away from Umuofia for seven years and he has come to live in a strange country. Because of this Okonkwo is very, very unhappy. But I want to ask him a question.'

Then Uchendu stopped and looked at Okonkwo.

'We all know that a man is head of his family,' said Uchendu. 'A man's wives do what he tells them to do. A child belongs to his father and his father's family. A child does not belong to his mother and her family. A man belongs to the country that his father comes from. He does not belong to the country that his mother comes from.'

'I know that this is true,' said Okonkwo.

'Then here is a question,' said Uchendu. 'Why do we often give our children the name "Nneka"? This word, "Nneka", means "Mother is most important of all". Why do we say "Mother is most important of all" when a child belongs to his father and a man to his father's country? Why do we say that?'

There was silence. Nobody spoke.

'I want Okonkwo to answer this question,' said Uchendu.

'I do not know the answer,' replied Okonkwo.

'You do not know the answer,' said Uchendu. 'So you see you are like a child. You have many wives and many children. You have more children than I have. You were an important man in your clan. But you are still like a child.'

Uchendu continued talking to Okonkwo.

'Now listen to me and I will tell you the answer,' said

Uchendu. 'But before I tell you, I want you to answer one more question. And this is the question: when a woman dies she is taken home to be buried with her own clan. She is not buried with her husband's clan. Why is this?'

Okonkwo shook his head because he did not know the answer.

'Okonkwo doesn't know the answer,' said Uchendu. 'He doesn't know the answers to my two questions.'

Then Uchendu turned to talk to his sons and daughters.

'Can any of you answer my questions?' Uchendu asked.

None of them could answer, so they shook their heads also.

'Then listen to me,' replied Uchendu. 'It's true that a child belongs to his father's country when everything in his life is happy. But when life is bad and unhappy, he goes to

47

his mother's country to be comforted. His mother is there to take care of him. She is buried there. And that is the reason for the idea that a "Mother is most important of all".'

Uchendu went on talking.

'Is it good, Okonkwo,' asked Uchendu, 'that when you came back to your mother's country, you should come with a sad face? You have made your mother unhappy and you won't let anyone comfort you. You should comfort your wives and your children while you are here, and then take them all back to Umuofia with you after seven years. But if you are unhappy all the time, you will die of unhappiness. And then who will look after your family?'

Uchendu stopped talking and waited for a little while. Then he pointed to his sons and daughters, and spoke to Okonkwo again.

'These people,' said Uchendu, 'are now your family. You think you are the most unhappy person in the whole world. You think you are the unluckiest person in the whole world. Do you know that sometimes men are sent away from their country for all their lives? Do you know that some men lose all their yams and even all their children?

'I had six wives once,' continued Uchendu. 'Now I have only one young wife and she is stupid. Do you know how many of my children have died? I have buried twenty-two children. I did not hang myself and I am still happy and alive. Other people in the world have troubles. You are not the only one. You should not walk about looking unhappy all the time and making other people unhappy too. So think about your life and yourself. I have no more to say to you.'

Uchendu was then silent. He got up and left the hut.

Okonkwo sat alone and thought about everything his uncle had said to him.

14

News Comes from Umuofia

After a year or more, Obierika, Okonkwo's friend, came from Umuofia to visit him. Obierika brought two young men. Each of the men carried a heavy bag on his head. Each bag was full of cowrie shells for Okonkwo.

Okonkwo was very happy to see his friend. And so were his wives and children. Then Okonkwo took the three men to meet Uchendu.

'You are all welcome,' said Uchendu to Obierika and his men. Then Uchendu offered them all some-kola nuts and palm wine.

The men started to talk about the clans and the villages they all knew. They talked about the clan at Abame.

'Have you heard that nearly all the people in Abame have been killed?' asked Obierika. 'There is no clan there any more.'

'Why is that?' asked Okonkwo, and everyone else together.

'Nearly everybody in Abame has been killed and everything destroyed,' said Obierika. 'It is a strange and a terrible story to tell you. I would not believe it, but I met one or two people who did not die and they told me what happened.'

And Obierika told them all the story.

'Three months ago,' said Obierika, 'a few men came into Umuofia. They were running away from Abame and they wanted to stay in Umuofia with us. They told us this terrible story.

'These men said that a white man had come to their village and . . .'

'You mean a man who was an albino[23]?' asked Okonkwo.

'He was not an albino. This man was different,' said Obierika, drinking his palm-wine.

'This man,' continued Obierika, 'was riding an iron horse. The first villagers who saw this white man ran away, but he waved to them and asked them to come and talk to him. Some of them went up to him and even touched his body.

'The important men in the clan asked the Oracle about the white man,' continued Obierika. 'The Oracle told them that this stranger would break up their clan and destroy it. The Oracle also said that more white men would come to Abame later on.'

Obierika took a drink of wine, and went on talking.

'Because of the words of the Oracle,' said Obierika, 'the clansmen killed this white stranger and tied his iron horse to a tree. They thought it might run away to tell the white man's friends.'

'What did the white man say before they killed him?' asked Uchendu.

'He said nothing,' answered one of the friends of Obierika.

'He said something, but nobody understood him,' said Obierika.

'One of the men told me,' said Obierika's other friend, 'that he repeated one word many times. That word sounded like Mbaino. Perhaps he was going to Mbaino and had lost his way.'

'Anyway,' continued Obierika, 'they killed this white man and tied his iron horse to a tree. For a long time, nothing happened. The iron horse was still tied to the tree. And then one morning, three white men came to the clan at Abame. They were led by a group of black men like us. Then they all went away.'

Everyone listened to the story Obierika was telling them. It was the most interesting news they had heard for a long time.

'Most of the men and women in Abame were working on their farms,' said Obierika, 'so only a few people saw these white men come into the village. For many weeks nothing else happened. Then one day, when nearly everyone in the clan was at the market, the three white men and some other men surrounded the market. They must have used a powerful medicine to stop people from seeing them until the market was full. Then the white men began to shoot at the people. Everyone in the village was killed except the old people and the sick people who had stayed at home.'

Obierika paused.

'The clan at Abame is now destroyed,' continued Obierika. 'No one is left there. Even the fish in the lake have gone away and the water in the lake has turned the colour of blood. Great destruction has come to Abame, as the Oracle had promised.'

There was a long silence, then suddenly Uchendu shouted.

'Never kill a man who says nothing,' said Uchendu. 'Those men at Abame were foolish. What did they know about the white man?'

'They were very foolish,' said Okonkwo, after another silence. 'The Oracle had told them that something bad was going to

51

happen. The people should have taken their guns and their matchets when they went to the market.'

'The people were foolish,' said Obierika. 'They have suffered because they were foolish. But I am very frightened. We have all heard stories about white men who make powerful guns and strong drinks and who take slaves across the sea. But no one thought these stories were true.'

'Every story is true,' replied Uchendu. 'Life is different for different people. Some things are good for some people and bad for others. We must believe what we hear about the white man.'

Okonkwo's first wife soon finished the cooking and gave the guests a big meal. Nwoye brought in a pot of fresh, sweet wine.

'You are a big man now,' Obierika said to Nwoye.

Ezinma brought in a bowl of water and everyone washed their hands. After that, they started to eat and drink. When they had finished the meal, Obierika pointed to the two heavy bags on the floor.

'That is the money for your yams,' he said to Okonkwo. 'I sold the big yams when you left, and later I sold some of the seed yams. I shall sell your yams every year for you until you return. I thought you would need the money now so I brought it. Who knows what might happen tomorrow? White men have already come to see us. Perhaps green men will come to our clan next and shoot us.'

Obierika laughed as he said these last words.

'Our gods will not let that happen,' replied Okonkwo. 'Thank you very much for coming to see us all here. I do not know how to thank you enough for bringing my money and the news about Abame.'

'Don't thank me,' replied Obierika. 'You are my best friend and it is a duty to come and see you.'

Then Obierika and his two friends left Okonkwo and went back to Umuofia.

15

The Missionaries Come to Mbanta

While Okonkwo and his family were living in Mbanta, the missionaries[24] arrived in the village. There were six of them and one of them was a white man.

Every man and woman came out of their compounds to see the white man. They had all heard stories about the first white man who had been killed at Abame and about his iron horse tied to a tree. And so everyone came to see this new white man.

When all the people had met in the village, the white man began to speak to them. He spoke in English and the people did not understand him.

But he had an interpreter with him to speak to the people. The interpreter repeated all the white man's words in their language.

This interpreter was from a different clan. He was not from Mbanta. But he told the people he was like them. He said he was an African. They could see he was an African because he was black and because he spoke a language they could understand.

This interpreter said the other four Africans with him were the brothers of the people in Mbanta. He said that the white man was also their brother because they were all the sons of God. He told the people of Mbanta about this new God, who had made all the world and all the men and women in the world.

He told the people of Mbanta that they prayed to gods made of wood and stone. He told them these gods were not true gods. The people in the crowd were surprised when he said this. They started whispering to each other.

The interpreter told them other things too. He told them about Heaven. This was a place high above the sky. God lived in Heaven. Good men and women who prayed to God went to Heaven when they died. They lived happily with God in Heaven.

But there was another terrible place deep under the ground. This place was called Hell. There was a huge fire burning in Hell. Bad men and women who prayed to gods made of wood or stone went to Hell when they died. They were burnt in the huge fire in Hell.

The interpreter then said, 'We have come to help you. The great God has sent us. You must stop worshipping your false gods and worship the true God. If you worship Him, then you will go to Heaven when you die.'

The people listened and became more and more surprised. Some of them were becoming interested in what the interpreter was saying.

One man asked the interpreter a question.

'Where is the white man's iron horse?' asked the man.

The black missionaries talked to each other for a few moments. They decided the man asking the question meant the white man's bicycle, when he talked about the iron horse. The missionaries told the white man about the question and he smiled gently.

'Tell them,' the white man said, 'that I shall bring many iron horses when we come to live in Mbanta. Many of the people will even ride the horses themselves.'

The interpreter told the people this but they did not listen. They were too busy talking to each other because the white man had said he was going to live in Mbanta. They had not thought about the white man coming to live among them.

At this moment an old man said he wanted to ask a question.

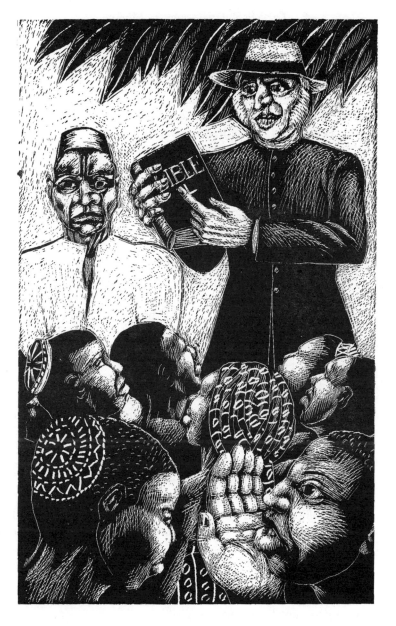

'You must stop worshipping your false gods and worship the true God.'

'Which is this god of yours?' he asked. 'Is it the goddess of the earth, or the god of the sky, or another god?'

The interpreter explained this question to the white man. Then the white man gave his answer. The interpreter explained to the people what the white man was saying.

'All the gods you have named are not gods at all,' said the white man. 'They're not true gods because they tell you to kill each other. Your gods tell you to kill your children if they are born as twins. There is only one true God and He made the earth, the sky, you and me and all of us.'

'What will happen if we leave our gods and follow your god?' asked another man. 'Who will keep us safe from the anger of the gods we have stopped worshipping?'

'Your gods are not alive and they cannot hurt you,' replied the white man. 'Your gods are only figures of wood and stone.'

When the men in Mbanta heard these words, they laughed and laughed at the white man. They thought to themselves that he must be mad. Any person must be mad to think that their gods could not hurt people.

Just then, the missionaries started singing a song – a happy song. The interpreter told the people what the song was about and everyone listened to the words. After the singing, the interpreter spoke about the Son of God whose name was Jesus Christ.

Okonkwo was in the crowd. He had listened to all the talking. He was not interested. He stayed at the meeting only because he wanted to chase the men away from the village with whips.

Then Okonkwo spoke to the interpreter.

'You told us just now that there is only one god,' said Okonkwo. 'Now you are talking about his son. Your god must have a wife then.'

The crowd listened and agreed with Okonkwo.

'I did not say He had a wife,' replied the interpreter.

'Yes you did. You said your god had a son called Jesus Christ. So your god must have a wife as well.'

Some of the people began to laugh.

The missionaries did not answer this question. They went on talking about more things the people did not believe. Okonkwo thought the interpreter must be very mad. Okonkwo left and went home to look at his palm trees.

But there was one young boy who had been listening very carefully to the missionaries. This boy was interested in the new religion, and his name was Nwoye. Nwoye did not understand everything the missionaries had said, but the song and the music had excited him.

After the death of Ikemefuna, Nwoye had become an unhappy and lonely boy. He did not understand many of the customs of his clan. He did not understand why his father had killed Ikemefuna. He did not like the custom of mothers throwing their twins into the forest to die. This new religion told Nwoye these customs were cruel and wicked. So Nwoye liked the new religion of the missionaries. He liked the new religion because it told you to love everybody.

Nwoye had never liked some of the customs of his clan. But he had never understood why he did not like the customs. Now this new religion was giving him some of the answers to his questions. Nwoye felt much happier inside. The words of the missionaries seemed to fill up some of the empty spaces he had inside him. Nwoye left the meeting that day and thought a lot about what he had heard. Something new and exciting had come into his life at last.

The Missionaries Build a Church

The missionaries spent the first four or five nights in the market-place. In the morning they told the people of Mbanta about God. They asked the people who the king of the village was, but the people replied that there was no king.

'We have our leaders and our priests and our wise men, but we do not have a king,' the people said.

At last the missionaries found the men who ruled Mbanta. The missionaries asked these rulers for a piece of land where they could build a church.

Every clan and village has its Evil Forest. If people died of a bad illness, they were buried in the Evil Forest. Nobody went into the Evil Forest because it was full of evil and dangerous spirits. The people believed that if anyone went into the Evil Forest he would die.

There was an Evil Forest in Mbanta. The rulers gave this forest to the missionaries to build their church.

'These missionaries want a piece of land to build a church,' said Uchendu. 'We shall give them a piece of land. We shall give them a part of the Evil Forest. These men believe their god will keep them safe. Let them prove it.'

The next morning, the missionaries began to cut down some of the trees in the Forest. Then they built a small house to live in. The people in Mbanta thought the missionaries would be all dead after four days.

But the first day passed, and the second day and the third, and then the fourth. Everyone was very, very surprised that all the missionaries were still alive. Nobody could understand why the missionaries had not died in the Evil Forest.

Slowly, the people began to believe that the white man's

religion had a special magic power. Soon three people from Mbanta started to worship the new God. They became the first three converts[25] in the village.

The new religion was called Christianity. The people who worshipped the new God were called Christians.

Nwoye liked the new religion. He had enjoyed listening to the missionaries talking about their God. But Nwoye did not tell anyone that he was interested. He dared not go too near the missionaries. If Okonkwo found out that Nwoye went to see the missionaries, he would beat his son very hard. But if the missionaries ever had a meeting in the open market-place or on the village playground, Nwoye went and listened to them. He soon learnt some of the stories the missionaries were telling the people.

The interpreter's name was Mr Kiaga. He was now in charge of the few people who had become converts. The white man had gone to Umuofia where he lived and worked.

'We have now built a church,' said Mr Kiaga to the converts. 'We want all of you to come to church every Sunday to worship the true God.'

The next Sunday, Nwoye walked past the church one way. Then he walked past it again the other way. The church was made of red earth and it had a roof made of straw. Nwoye wanted to go inside the church but he was too frightened. He heard the converts singing loudly and happily. Nwoye was very frightened because the church was built in the Evil Forest. At last, he left the Forest and went home.

The people in Mbanta knew that their gods were kind. But the people also knew that the gods would be kind for only a short time. Soon the missionaries and the converts would be punished. The gods would punish the missionaries before seven weeks were over.

When the seventh week came, the people got more and more excited. They were sure their gods would punish these missionaries at the end of seven weeks.

At last the day came when all the missionaries should have died. But they were all still alive. The missionaries were now building a new house for their interpreter and teacher, Mr Kiaga. The people could not believe it. The new religion had power. A few more people began to believe the new religion and they became converts too. One of the new converts was a woman—the first woman in Mbanta to become a Christian.

17

Nwoye Leaves his Home

One morning, a cousin of Okonkwo was walking past the church. He saw Nwoye with the other converts. He was very surprised and when he got home he told Okonkwo. When Okonkwo heard the news he sat silently and did not move.

Nwoye returned home late in the afternoon. He went to his father's hut to greet him, but Okonkwo did not answer. Nwoye turned round to walk away out of the hut. Suddenly Okonkwo became very, very angry. He jumped up, ran to Nwoye, and held him by his neck.

'Where have you been?' Okonkwo shouted at Nwoye.

Nwoye tried to get free from his father's hands, but he could not.

'Answer me,' shouted Okonkwo again, very loudly.

Nwoye stood and looked at his father. He did not say anything. Okonkwo's wives stood outside the hut. They screamed loudly when they heard Okonkwo beating Nwoye but they were too frightened to go inside.

'Let that boy go at once,' said a man's voice outside the hut.

It was the voice of Uchendu, Okonkwo's uncle.

'Why do you beat Nwoye like that?' he asked.

Okonkwo did not answer. But he let Nwoye go free. Nwoye walked out of the hut and never went home again.

Nwoye went back to the church. He told Mr Kiaga that he had left his home and was going to Umuofia. In Umuofia the white missionary had started a school to teach young Christians to read and write.

When Nwoye told Mr Kiaga that he wanted to go to Umuofia, Mr Kiaga was very happy. Nwoye was happy, too, because he was going to leave his father. He decided he would return later to his mother and his brothers and convert them to the new religion as well.

Okonkwo sat in his hut the night Nwoye left home. He looked into the fire and thought about Nwoye and the new religion. Suddenly Okonkwo felt very angry. He wanted to go to the church and kill all the converts with his matchet. But then Okonkwo told himself that Nwoye was not worth fighting for.

Why, Okonkwo asked himself, should I have a son who is so bad and so weak? Why has my son left the gods of his own clan? Why is he going with a lot of weak men who talk like a lot of girls?

Then Okonkwo remembered his own father Unoka. Nwoye was weak like a girl. So was Nwoye's grandfather.

When I was Nwoye's age, Okonkwo said to himself, I was famous in all Umuofia for my wrestling and my fighting.

Okonkwo felt very sad when he thought about his weak son. He was ashamed of Nwoye. Now Nwoye had left his family, Okonkwo would forget him. Okonkwo knew that he would never see his son again.

18

Some New Converts

When the church was built in Mbanta, the missionaries did not have any big problems. At first, the people thought that the converts would get bored quickly with the new religion. They thought that the converts would return to worship their own gods. But they did not and more and more people in the clan became Christians.

The clan did not worry too much. Most of the converts were unimportant people, and they did no harm living in the Evil

Forest. Sometimes, in the forest, converts found twins which had been thrown away by their mothers. The converts brought the twins back to their own huts but they never took them into the village.

No one wanted to kill any of the missionaries. The clan thought the missionaries were mad, but they also thought they were harmless. And no one would kill a convert. The converts were unimportant people, but they still belonged to the clan. If anyone killed a convert he would have to leave the clan. If the Christians started to make trouble, then the people would chase them away. But they would not kill the converts.

But slowly, the missionaries and the converts began to have problems. And these problems were caused by people who were called *osu*.

An *osu* is a person who follows a different god. He cannot marry an ordinary person. He has to have his hair long and dirty. An *osu* can never be a ruler in the clan. When he dies, he is buried in the Evil Forest. Ordinary people must not talk to an *osu* and an *osu* is excluded[26] from the clan.

The trouble between the missionaries and the converts began when the *osu* people wanted to become converts. The *osu* saw that the new religion invited twins into the church, so they thought they would be welcome, too.

So, one Sunday, *two* osu went into the church. The converts were very surprised but they did not leave the church when the *osu* went in. They just moved away and sat a long way from the *osu*.

None of the converts said anything until the end of the singing and the prayers. Then they all said that the *osu* people could not come into the church and they started driving the *osu* away. But Mr Kiaga stopped them.

'We are all God's children,' said Mr Kiaga, 'and everybody is our brother. Even these *osu* people are our brothers.'

'You don't understand,' said one of the converts. 'What will

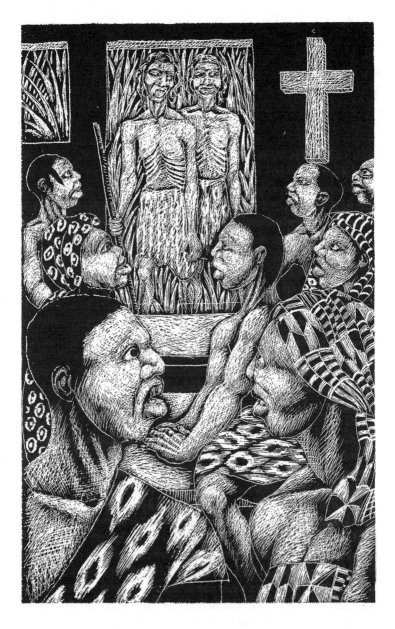

One Sunday, two osu went into the church.

the villagers say about us when they hear that we are inviting the *osu* into our church? The villagers will laugh and make fun of us.'

'Let the villagers laugh at us,' replied Mr Kiaga. 'God will laugh at the villagers when they die and go to Hell.'

'You don't understand,' said the convert again. 'You are our teacher and you can teach us the things about the new religion. But we know about the *osu* people and we must not mix with them.'

'An *osu* needs God more than you do,' said Mr Kiaga.

Then he told the converts that they must let the *osu* into the church if they wanted to come in. He told the converts that Christianity is a religion of love. Christians must love both twins and *osu*.

'Then I shall go back to the clan,' said the convert.

Mr Kiaga said nothing. So the convert left and went back to his clansmen. Mr Kiaga did not try to stop him. He had to make sure that his converts really believed that all men are equal and are brothers.

Mr Kiaga told the *osu* people to cut off their long, dirty hair. At first they thought they would die if they cut off their hair, so they refused.

'Unless you cut off your hair,' said Mr Kiaga, 'I will not let any of you come into the church. You are not *osu* any more. You are Christians and you must believe what I tell you.'

The *osu* looked at him. They did not know what to do.

'Why do you think you will die if you cut your hair off?' Mr Kiaga asked them. 'Are you different from other men who cut their hair? The same God made you and them. But your brothers in the clan have chased you away from the clan. They say that you will die if you cut your hair off. They said I would die if I built the church in the Evil Forest. Am I dead? They also said that I would die if I looked after twins. I've looked after twins, and I am still alive. People who don't believe in my God speak only lies. Only the words of God are true.'

65

So the two *osu* cut off their long, dirty hair and soon they were two of the best converts in the church. And nearly all the other *osu* in Mbanta followed them and became Christians as well.

19

The Death of a Holy Snake

A year later one of the *osu*, who was a convert, was in trouble with the clan in Mbanta. The trouble started because this *osu* killed a holy snake.

Everyone believed that the holy snake came from the god of water. The holy snake was the most respected animal in Mbanta. The snake was called 'Our Father', and it could go anywhere it wanted to go. It could even go into people's beds. Nobody would stop it.

If a clansman killed the snake by accident, he had to say special prayers to the gods and he gave the animal an expensive burial. Nobody thought that a man would kill a holy snake on purpose and so no one had ever heard about a punishment for killing it.

Nobody saw this *osu* kill the snake, but everyone thought he had killed it. The rulers of Mbanta met to decide what to do. Some of them were very angry. Okonkwo said there would never be any peace in Mbanta until all the worthless Christians had been chased away from the village with whips. Some of the other rulers did not agree with Okonkwo.

'Nobody saw the *osu* kill the snake,' they said. 'If a man kills this animal secretly in his own hut, only the gods can punish him. If we punish him, then the gods might punish us. This is wise. So we will not punish him.'

Okonkwo did not agree with these rulers.

'These converts are making this clan weaker and weaker,' said Okonkwo. 'We are all becoming cowards.'

'Okonkwo is speaking the truth,' said another man. 'We must do something. Let us exclude these Christians from the clan. Then the gods will not think that we agree with the things they do.'

Everyone at the meeting spoke. In the end they all agreed not to let the Christians take any part in the life of the clan any more. Okonkwo felt ashamed of the clan in Mbanta. His own clan in Umuofia would not be so weak and cowardly as this clan in Mbanta.

The next day was a Wednesday. It was the Wednesday in Holy Week. This was the most important week of the year for Christians.

Mr Kiaga had asked the women converts to bring red earth and white chalk and water to clean the church. The women had made three groups for the cleaning. One group went to the stream to get water in their pots. The second group went to collect red earth in their baskets. And the third group went to find chalk.

Mr Kiaga was praying in the church when he heard the women talking excitedly outside. He went to see what was happening. The women had come to the church with empty water pots. They said that some men had chased them away from the stream with whips.

Soon after that, the women who had gone for red earth returned with empty baskets. Some of them had been whipped badly. The women who had gone for chalk came back with empty baskets as well.

'What does all this mean?' asked Mr Kiaga, who was very worried.

'The clan has excluded us from doing things in the village,' said one of the women. 'The people of the clan will not let us take water from the stream.'

'The clan wants to make our lives difficult,' said another woman. 'They will not let us go to market.'

'Come with us,' the men said to the women. 'We will go with you to meet these people who have stopped you getting water.'

But Mr Kiaga stopped the converts leaving. He wanted to know why the converts had been excluded from the clan.

'The clan says that the new *osu* convert killed the holy snake,' said one man.

'It's not true,' said another. 'The *osu* told me he did not kill it.'

Nobody could find out the truth about the snake. The new *osu* convert was not there. He had become ill the night before and he died very quickly. His death showed the clan that the gods had punished him for killing the snake.

Now the *osu* was dead, the clan did not have any reason to exclude the converts from the clan. The Christians were once again allowed back in to the clan.

20

Okonkwo Returns to Umuofia

The seven years Okonkwo and his family spent in Mbanta finished at last. Okonkwo could now return to Umuofia.

Before Okonkwo left Mbanta he prepared a large meal. He wanted to thank his mother for looking after him and his family. A lot of important people came to the big meal and everybody enjoyed it.

When Okonkwo got back to his village in Umuofia, he wanted all his own clansmen to notice him. He wanted them to think he was still an important person. So Okonkwo built a very large compound. It was much bigger than his first one. He built a bigger barn. And he built huts for his two new wives.

Okonkwo hoped everyone in Umuofia would still respect him. He still wanted to be one of the leaders of the clan.

Umuofia had changed a lot during the seven years Okonkwo had been away. The new religion had also come to Umuofia and the missionaries had built a church. Many people had become converts. The clan did not worry because most of the converts were unimportant people. But one or two converts were important men in the clan. The missionary was proud of these important men who gave up their own gods to follow the Christian God.

The white missionary had brought religion to Umuofia. Another white man, called the District Commissioner, brought a new kind of government. The Commissioner built a new court. In the court he judged people who disobeyed the new laws.

This Commissioner also had messengers to find men who broke the white man's law.

Most of the messengers came from another part of Africa. The people in Umuofia hated these messengers because they were strangers and because they were proud. The messengers thought they were better than the people of Umuofia. They did not follow the laws of Umuofia.

These messengers guarded the prison. Inside the prison were many clansmen who had broken the new law of the white man. The messengers used to beat the men in prison. The prisoners were forced to clean the Commissioner's compound and collect wood for his fires.

When Okonkwo heard that some of the important men in the clan were in prison, he was very sad.

'Perhaps I have been away from Umuofia too long,' Okonkwo

said. 'I cannot understand the things I hear. What has happened to our clan? Why cannot our people fight in the way they used to fight in the past?

'Why has everyone become weak?' Okonkwo asked his friends.

Then Okonkwo's friend, Obierika, spoke.

'Have you not heard how the white man destroyed everything

in Abame?' asked Obierika. 'I think I told you when I came to see you in Mbanta.'

'Yes, you did,' replied Okonkwo. 'But the people in Abame were weak and foolish. Why didn't they fight back? Didn't they have guns and matchets to use? We must not be weak like the people in Abame. We must fight these white men and chase them away from our country.'

'It's too late to do that,' replied Obierika sadly. 'Our own men have joined the white man's religion and they like the white man's government. We could easily drive the white men away from our country. There are only two white men – the missionary and the commissioner. But what could we do with our own clansmen who have become converts? If we fought the converts, they would bring soldiers. These soldiers would destroy Umuofia as they destroyed Abame.

'The white man is very clever,' continued Obierika. 'He came to our country quietly and peacefully with his new religion. We thought he was foolish so we laughed at him and we let him live among us. Now many of our clansmen follow his religion and his laws. Once our leaders and our own religion held our people together. Now the white man has broken up the clan. Our clan is falling apart.'

Obierika stopped talking. Both he and Okonkwo sat in silence. They were too sad to say any more. They both knew that the white man was beginning to control Umuofia with his religion and his laws.

21

The Rule of the White Man Grows

Most people in Umuofia thought that the white man's religion was mad. They thought it was mad, so they did not worry about it too much. The white man had brought religion with him but he had also brought trade. Umuofia was getting rich. It was selling crops to other countries.

Mr Brown, the white missionary, was a kind man. He told his converts not to make the other people in the clan angry. He told them not to say bad things about the gods of the clan. Mr Brown did not make everyone become a Christian. Nearly everybody in the clan liked him and respected him. Some of the important clansmen became his friends and they often gave him presents because they liked him.

Mr Brown used to have long talks with some of the clansmen. He learnt a lot about the old religions of the clan. He decided that he could not make everyone become a Christian and worship his God. So he decided to change the people slowly.

Mr Brown built a school and a little hospital. He went round from family to family asking people to send their children to his new school. At first, they sent only their slaves and sometimes their lazy children.

Mr Brown told the people it was very important to read and write. He said that soon the leaders of the clan would be people who could read and write. If people in Umuofia did not send their children to school to learn, then strangers would come from other countries and rule them.

Slowly more and more people went to the school. Not all the students were children. Some of the students were thirty years old. Some were even older.

These men worked on their farms in the mornings and went

to school in the afternoons. After a few months at school, some of them became court messengers or even court clerks. Those students who stayed at the school for a longer time became teachers.

Slowly new churches were built in the little villages around Umuofia and new schools were started. Mr Brown worked very hard. More and more of the clansmen became converts.

One day, Mr Brown went to see Okonkwo. He wanted to tell Okonkwo about his son, Nwoye. Nwoye now had the Christian name of Isaac. He was a convert and he had gone to a new college for teachers. Mr Brown hoped Okonkwo would be happy to know the news about his son.

But Okonkwo was not happy. Instead Okonkwo was very angry and he chased Mr Brown away from his compound. Okonkwo told him that if he came back again he would give Mr Brown a beating.

Okonkwo was not happy in Umuofia. Nobody took any notice of him when he returned. The clan had changed a lot in the seven years. Most people were interested in the new religion or the new government or the new trading places. They talked about the new way of life in Umuofia. They talked a lot about the good things the white men had brought with them. But they did not talk about the bravery of Okonkwo any more.

This made Okonkwo very sad. He was sad because nobody noticed him very much. He was also sad because his clan was breaking up and falling apart. They had become soft and weak like women. They had all changed. These changes were made by the white men. Okonkwo began to hate these white men in his country.

A little later, Mr Brown became ill and he had to leave Umuofia for ever. The man who came after him was called Mr Smith.

Mr Smith was very different from Mr Brown. Mr Smith did not like the African people and he was always rude to them.

One day, there was a meeting of all the leaders of the clan. The leaders met to give thanks to the Earth Goddess. They dressed up in special clothes and wore masks on their faces.

One of the converts, called Enoch, said rude things about the leaders at the meeting. One of the clan hit Enoch with a stick and Enoch hit him back and tore off the man's mask.

The clan was very angry. Enoch had taken off a leader's mask at a very important religious meeting. The clansmen decided to punish Enoch. The next day, some of them went to his compound. The converts knew the clansmen would attack Enoch, so Mr Smith hid Enoch in his own house.

The clansmen went to Enoch's compound. They set fire to his huts and burnt them down. Then, still angry and excited, they went to the church. Mr Smith was in the church. He heard the men coming so he went to meet them at the door. Mr Smith's interpreter stood behind him.

'Tell the white man we will not harm him,' said one of the clansmen. 'Tell the white man to go back to his house and leave us alone.'

Mr Smith and the interpreter just looked at the clansman. Then the same man spoke again.

'We liked Mr Brown,' said the clansman. 'Mr Brown was foolish, but we liked him. Because we liked him, we will not harm his friend here,' the clansman said. 'But we must burn the church down. The church has given us many problems so we have come to destroy it.'

Then the clansman spoke to Mr Smith.

'You can stay here in Umuofia with us if you want to,' he said. 'You can worship your own God if you want to. But you must worship Him in your own house. You must not convert any more of our people to your religion. Go back to your house. We are very, very angry, but we will not harm you.'

Mr Smith listened to this speech, and then he spoke to his interpreter.

'Tell them to go away from here,' he said. 'The church is the house of God. I will not let the church be destroyed by people who don't believe in my religion.'

The interpreter was frightened of the clansmen, so he did not tell them what Mr Smith had said. Instead he told a lie.

'The white man says he is happy you have come to tell him your problems. He will be happy if you let him decide what to do,' the interpreter replied.

'We can't let him decide what to do,' said one of the leaders. 'He does not understand our way of life and we don't understand his way of life. Tell him to go away.'

The clansmen were very angry. They had come to burn the church down. So they set fire to the church and soon it was burning.

Mr Smith did not go home. He stood and watched the church

which Mr Brown had built, burning to the ground.

The clansmen went away happy. They had punished the Christians for taking the mask off one of their leaders at the meeting. They thought the Christians would not make any more trouble in Umuofia.

22

Okonkwo is Put in Prison

After the clan had burnt down the church in Umuofia, Okonkwo was very, very happy. He was happier than he had been for many years. His clan was once again strong and brave. His people were not afraid of the Christians any more. They had not killed the white man, but they had burnt down his church. They had told the white man that he must not try to convert any more clansmen to the new religion.

For two days after the burning of the church, nothing happened. Every man in Umuofia walked about with a gun or a matchet. They were not going to be foolish like the people of Abame. The people of Abame had all been killed because they did not have guns or matchets when the white man came.

Then the Commissioner returned to Umuofia. He was away visiting another village when the clan burnt the church. When the Commissioner got back, Mr Smith told him what had happened.

Three days later, the Commissioner sent a polite messenger to the leaders of Umuofia. The messenger asked the leaders to meet the Commissioner in his office. Okonkwo was one of the six leaders who went to see the Commissioner.

The six leaders went to the Commissioner's office. They took their matchets with them, but they left their guns at home. The Commissioner met them politely.

'I have asked you to come,' he said to the leaders, 'to talk about the burning of the church. I was not in Umuofia when it happened. Mr Smith told me about it, but I cannot believe his story until you have told me what happened.'

The Commissioner paused.

'Let us be friends,' he said. 'I don't want to hear that any more churches have been burnt down ever again.'

One of the leaders stood up and started to tell the story.

'Wait a minute,' said the Commissioner. 'I want to bring in my men so that they can hear what you say.'

'Go and bring in my men,' the Commissioner said to his interpreter.

The interpreter left the room and came back with twelve men. They all sat down and the leader began to tell his story again.

Just as the leader began to speak, the twelve men suddenly jumped up and tied together the hands of the six leaders. It was done so quickly that the leaders did not have time to pick up their matchets. When the messengers had tied the leaders' hands together, they took them to another room.

Then the Commissioner spoke to them.

'We shall not hurt you,' he said, 'but you must agree to help us. I have brought a good government to your country to make your people happy and peaceful. If any man hurts you, I will help you. But I will not let you hurt anyone else.'

The six leaders said nothing, so the Commissioner continued.

'You burnt down Enoch's compound. Then you burnt down the church. I must punish you for doing these things. As a punishment you must give the court two hundred bags of cowrie shells. When you have done this, I will let you all go free,' the Commissioner said.

The leaders still said nothing, so the Commissioner spoke to them. 'What do you want to say?' he asked.

The six leaders sat in silence. They did not speak. The Commissioner told his men to look after the six men well as they were the leaders of Umuofia. The messengers said, 'Yes, Sir,' and the Commissioner went away.

When the Commissioner had gone, one of the messengers got a razor and cut off the hair of all the leaders. The leaders' hands were still tied together so they could not fight. They sat and looked miserable.

The six leaders refused to eat any food for two days. The messengers did not give them any water to drink. At night the messengers went into the prison to laugh at the men and to bang their heads together. On the third day, the men were very, very hungry. They began to talk to each other. They talked about getting the cowrie shells from the clansmen so that they could go free.

'We should have killed the white man,' said Okonkwo.

'Who wants to kill the white man?' asked a messenger, who heard what Okonkwo had said.

Nobody spoke. The messenger had a very thick stick in his hand. He hit each man on his head and his back many times. Okonkwo was very angry. He was so angry he could not speak.

As soon as the messengers had locked up the six men that day, they went to the people of Umuofia. They told the people that the Commissioner would not free their leaders until they gave the court two hundred and fifty bags of cowrie shells.

'If you don't give the cowrie shells immediately,' said one of the messengers, 'we will hang your leaders.'

Soon, everyone in the villages heard the news about the leaders of Umuofia. Everyone was frightened. Everyone stayed in their huts. No one went out to visit friends that night. None of the children played on the village green in the moonlight.

The only noise was the voice of the town-crier. He walked slowly round the villages of Umuofia. He hit his gong and told every man to go to a meeting in the market-place in the morning. The crier walked from one end of Umuofia to the other. Everyone heard what he said.

The next morning, the men of Umuofia went to the market–place. They agreed to give the white man two hundred and fifty bags of cowrie shells immediately.

The men of Umuofia did not know that fifty of these bags would be taken by the court messengers. The white man had asked for two hundred bags but his messengers asked the people for two hundred and fifty bags. The messengers would keep the other fifty bags for themselves.

23

Okonkwo Kills a Messenger

The people of Umuofia gave the cowries to the messengers. Then Okonkwo and the five other leaders were let out of prison.

Okonkwo went back to his compound. Ezinma cooked some food for him. Okonkwo ate it but he was not hungry. He was still very angry.

Okonkwo's family and friends were in his hut with him. Obierika told Okonkwo to eat up all the food. Nobody else spoke. Okonkwo's friends saw the long marks on Okonkwo's back. The court messengers had made these marks when they had beaten him.

The town-crier walked around the village of Umuofia again that night. He hit his gong and told the people that there was another meeting in the morning. Everyone knew that at last the people of Umuofia were going to speak angrily about the white man and the Christians.

Okonkwo did not sleep much that night. He was still very angry, but he was also excited. He was looking forward to the morning. Before he went to bed, he unpacked his war clothes. Okonkwo had not looked at his war clothes since he had come back to his village in Umuofia. He looked at his straw skirt and his hat with its large feather. He decided they were still good enough to use.

As Okonkwo lay on his bed he thought about the cruel way the white man had treated him. He decided to punish the white man for what had happened. Okonkwo would be happy if the people of Umuofia decided to go to war with the white man. But if the people of Umuofia were too frightened to fight, then he would fight alone. Okonkwo lay on his bed thinking what he would say to the people in the morning. Slowly he went to sleep.

————

As the sun rose, people began to go to the market-place. Okonkwo went to meet Obierika, and the two men walked together to the market. When they got there the market-place was full, but more and more people kept arriving. Okonkwo was very happy to see so many clansmen at the meeting.

Then a man stood up and shouted a greeting to the people.

'Umuofia kwenu,' he shouted. These words mean, 'We greet you, Umuofia.' The man then raised his left hand high in the air.

'Yaa,' all the people shouted back.

'Umuofia kwenu,' the man shouted again.

Each time the man shouted these words, he faced a different direction. Each time the crowd shouted back, 'Yaa'.

Then everyone was silent. Another man, called Okika, stood up and began to speak.

'You all know why we are here,' Okika said. 'All our gods are crying. They are crying because our clansmen have made them unhappy.'

Okika stopped. His voice was shaking. Then he continued.

'This is a great meeting,' said Okika, 'but are all the men of Umuofia here?' he asked. 'Are all the men of Umuofia meeting together in agreement?'

When the crowd heard Okika say this, they began to talk quietly to each other.

'No. They are not all here,' continued Okika. 'Some of our men have left the clan and follow the white man's way of life. We follow the way of life of our fathers. The men who are not here have left us now and follow a stranger in their own country.'

Okika paused, and looked at the crowd. Then he went on.

'If we fight this stranger, this white man, we shall also fight our clansmen who follow him,' said Okika. 'We shall be fighting our own people. But we must fight the white man. We must fight our own people who follow him. We must drive away this white man and his new religion. We must fight now.'

At that moment, there was a sudden movement in the crowd and everyone looked in the same direction. Five court messengers were standing a few feet from the crowd. Nobody had seen them arrive. They had come silently.

Okonkwo was sitting near them. He jumped to his feet immediately and stood in front of the chief messenger. Okonkwo was shaking with anger and hate. He could not speak. The messenger stood still and looked at Okonkwo. The other four messengers stood behind their friend. The crowd was silent. Nobody spoke a word.

'Let me come past,' the chief messenger said at last.

'What do you want here?' asked Okonkwo.

'I have come with a message from the white man,' the messenger replied. 'The white man says that you must stop this meeting at once.'

Suddenly Okonkwo lifted his matchet. The messenger saw that Okonkwo was going to hit him. The messenger bent down to escape from Okonkwo's matchet but he was too late. Okonkwo brought down his matchet twice, and the messenger's head lay on the ground beside his body.

The people in the crowd ran in all directions. The meeting was stopped. Okonkwo stood and looked at the dead messenger. Okonkwo knew then that the people of Umuofia would not fight the white man. Okonkwo knew it because they had let the other four messengers run away. He heard some men talking.

'Why did Okonkwo kill the messenger?' they asked each other.

Okonkwo then knew that he was alone. He was alone without his clan. He was still brave and strong but his clan was weak and cowardly. He had fought the white man by himself. His clansmen were cowards. The white man had broken up the clan. His people had fallen apart. The clan did not agree any more.

Okonkwo wiped his matchet after he had killed the messenger, and walked away.

24

The Death of Okonkwo

The four messengers who had run away from the meeting went straight to the Commissioner. They told the Commissioner that Okonkwo had killed their friend. Then the Commissioner went with some soldiers and his messengers to Okonkwo's compound.

When the Commissioner arrived at the compound, he ordered the men in Okonkwo's hut to come outside. They got up and went outside.

'Which one of you is called Okonkwo?' asked the Commissioner.

'Okonkwo is not here,' replied Obierika.

'Where is he?' asked the Commissioner.

'Okonkwo is not here,' Obierika said again.

The Commissioner became angry. His face went red. He told the men that he wanted to see Okonkwo immediately. He said they must give Okonkwo to him, or he would lock all of them up in the prison.

The men spoke quietly to each other. Then Obierika spoke.

'We can take you to where Okonkwo is, and perhaps your men can help us,' he said.

The Commissioner did not understand what Obierika meant when he said, 'Perhaps your men can help us.'

'Follow us,' said Obierika, and he led the way.

The Commissioner and his soldiers followed. The soldiers carried guns. The Commissioner told the soldiers to shoot Obierika and his men if they tried to run away.

Obierika led the men to a place just outside one of the walls of Okonkwo's compound. Then they came to a tree. Okonkwo's body was hanging from the tree. Okonkwo knew that the white man would hang him if he found him alive. So Okonkwo had decided to hang himself.

'Perhaps your men can help us cut Okonkwo's body down from the tree. And perhaps they can bury him,' said Obierika. 'We have sent for strangers from another village. We have asked them to come and cut him down, but they may not come for a long time.'

'Why can't you take the body down yourselves?' the Commissioner asked.

'It is against our laws,' replied one of the men. 'It is a crime for a man to kill himself. It is a crime against the Earth Goddess, and the man who kills himself cannot be buried by his own clansmen. His body is bad and only strangers can touch it.'

Obierika looked at the Commissioner and his men.

'You are strangers in Umuofia,' Obierika said. 'That is why we are asking you to cut down Okonkwo's body from the tree.'

'Will you bury him like any other man?' asked the Commissioner.

'We cannot bury him,' replied Obierika. 'Only strangers can bury a man who has killed himself.'

Obierika stopped talking and looked at the body of his friend hanging from the tree.

'We will pay your men to cut Okonkwo's body down and to bury him,' Obierika said. 'When you have buried him, we will ask the Earth Goddess to make the land clean again.'

Obierika suddenly turned to look at the Commissioner. Then he screamed out loudly, with great anger in his voice.

'That man hanging there,' shouted Obierika, 'was one of the

greatest men in Umuofia. You made him kill himself and now he will be buried like a dog . . .'

Obierika's voice shook with anger. He was so angry and so miserable that he could not say any more.

'Keep quiet,' shouted one of the messengers to Obierika.

'Take the body down,' said the Commissioner to the chief messenger. 'Bring the body of Okonkwo and all these people to the court.'

'Yes, sir,' replied the messenger.

So they cut down the hanging body of Okonkwo and carried him on their shoulders to the court of the white man.

Points for Understanding

1

1 What district did Okonkwo live in?
2 Why was Okonkwo ashamed of his father, Unoka?
3 Why did the clan respect Okonkwo?

2

1 Why were the other districts afraid of Umuofia?
2 What happened to Ikemefuna?

3

1 Why did Okonkwo keep beating Nwoye?
2 Why was Nwoye pleased when Ikemefuna came to live with
  Okonkwo's family?
3 Why did Okonkwo never let anyone see that he was kind?

4

1 How did Okonkwo break the rules of the Week of Peace?
2 Why did Ezeani tell Okonkwo to take certain things to the shrine
  of the Earth Goddess?
3 Why did Okonkwo not tell anyone that he was sorry?
4 Why were the other villagers not pleased with Okonkwo?

5

1 Why were the first two days of the New Year so important?
2 Why was Ekwefi so excited when she heard the drums?

6

1 Why was Okonkwo happy when Nwoye complained about the
  women?
2 What sort of stories did Nwoye like to listen to?
3 What was going to happen to Ikemefuna?
4 What did Ezeudu tell Okonkwo not to do?

87

7

1 How had Okonkwo broken one of the rules of the clan?
2 How did Nwoye feel when he was sure that Ikemefuna had been killed?
3 When did Nwoye lose his love for Okonkwo?

8

1 Why did Okonkwo think that he had become like a woman?
2 Why did Okonkwo wish that he had a son like Maduka?
3 How did Okonkwo feel after he had talked to Obierika?

9

1 Why did Ekwefi love Ezinma so much?
2 Ezinma was an *ogbanje*. What does that mean?

10

1 Who was Chielo?
2 Where did Chielo want to take Ezinma?
3 What did Ekwefi decide to do when Chielo took Ezinma away?

11

1 How did the priestess, Chielo, get in and out of the cave of the god, Agbala?
2 Why were Ekwefi and Okonkwo happy that Ezinma had gone into the cave of the god, Agbala?

12

1 Was the death of Ezeudu's son an accident?
2 What was the difference between a 'male' crime and a 'female' crime?
3 What was Okonkwo's punishment?
4 Where was Okonkwo going to go?
5 What happened to Okonkwo's compound?

13

1 Where did Okonkwo go to in Mbanta?
2 What had always been Okonkwo's one big wish?
3 Did Okonkwo think this wish would ever come true now?
4 What did Uchendu mean when he said, 'Mother is most
   important of all'?
5 What was Uchendu's advice to Okonkwo?

14

1 Who was the stranger at Abame and how did he come there?
2 What did the Oracle tell the people of Abame about this
   stranger?
3 Was the Oracle right?
4 Why did Okonkwo think the people of Abame were foolish?
5 Was Obierika afraid of the stories about the white men?
6 Was Okonkwo afraid of the white men?

15

1 Why did the interpreter say the missionaries had come to
   Mbanta?
2 What did the missionary say about the gods of the clan?
3 Why did Okonkwo stay at the meeting?
4 Why did Nwoye stay?

16

1 Why did Nwoye not go too near the missionaries?
2 What did the people of Mbanta think when the missionaries did
   not die in the Evil Forest?

17

1 Why did Okonkwo beat Nwoye?
2 What did Nwoye do when Okonkwo beat him?
3 What did Nwoye want to do in Umuofia?
4 Why did Okonkwo remember his father, Unoka?

18

1 Why did the clansmen not worry very much about the people who became converts?
2 Why did no one want to kill the missionaries?
3 How many of the *osu* became converts?

19

1 Why was Okonkwo ashamed of the clan in Mbanta?
2 Did the rulers of Mbanta continue to exclude the Christians?

20

1 Why did Okonkwo build a very large compound when he returned to Umuofia?
2 How had Umuofia changed since Okonkwo had left it?
3 What had the District Commissioner brought to Umuofia?
4 Who helped the District Commissioner in his work?
5 Why was Okonkwo sad when he returned to Umuofia?
6 What did Okonkwo want to do to the white men?
7 Why did Obierika think that it was too late to save Umuofia?

21

1 What had the white man brought to Umuofia as well as religion and government?
2 Why did Mr Brown build a school?
3 Okonkwo was unhappy in Umuofia for two reasons. One reason was that many people in the clan had accepted the white man and had become weak. What was the other reason?
4 What did the clansmen think when they burnt the Church?

22

1 Why was Okonkwo happy after the burning of the church?
2 The Commissioner said he had brought a good government to Umuofia. How does this chapter show that it was an unfair and dishonest government?
3 How powerful was the new government in Umuofia?
4 What did Okonkwo want to do to the white man now?

23

1 Some men of Umuofia were not at the meeting. Who were they?
2 What did Okonkwo do to the chief messenger at the meeting?
3 How did Okonkwo know that the men of Umuofia would not fight the white man?
4 What had happened to the clan?

24

1 Why did Obierika want the Commissioner's men to help him?
2 What did Obierika say about Okonkwo?
3 What do you think was the reason for Okonkwo's death?

Glossary

1 *customs* (page 4)
   the ways of life of a group of people, which make them different
   from other people. For example, their way of arranging marriages,
   cooking and eating food, burying people etc.

2 **wrestler** (page 7)
   to wrestle is to fight a man by holding him and pushing him to
   the ground. A wrestler is a man who fights in this way. (See the
   illustration on page 21)

3 **bush fire** (page 8)
   a fire which moves very quickly from one tree to another.

4 *palm wine* (page 8)
   an alcoholic drink which comes from a palm tree. *To tap a palm
   tree* is to make a hole in the tree to take out the liquid in the tree.
   The liquid is made into wine.

5 *be ashamed of someone* (page 8)
   to feel unhappy because someone important to you, like you or
   your mother, does foolish things.

6 *yam* (page 9)
   a large vegetable which grows in the ground. It is like a very large
   potato. It makes very good food.

7 *respect someone* (page 9)
   to be polite to someone because he or she works hard and does
   well. To think very well of a person.

8 *goatskin bag* (page 14)
   the skin of a goat is taken very carefully from the dead animal.
   The legs are carefully closed and the skin is made into a bag for
   holding things.

9 *priest/priestess* (page 16)
   a man or woman who is a special servant of a god. They clean the
   place where the image of the god is kept. They do the things that
   the god tells them to do. They also tell the people what the god
   wants them to do.

10 *kola-nuts* (page 16)
   nuts from the kola tree in West Africa. It is a custom to break
   and share the nuts with visitors and guests to show that they are
   welcome.

11 *evil* (page 17)
   something very bad which is against the laws of the gods.

12 **cowrie shells** (page 17)
    special small shells which were once used as money among people
    in parts of Africa and India.
13 **Oracle** (page 24)
    a god who speaks to the people through the mouth of its priest or
    priestess and tells the people what to do.
14 **matchet** (page 25)
    a sharp knife (see illustration on page 26).
15 **twins** (page 28)
    two children born at the same time from one mother.
16 **Evil Forest** (page 28)
    a bad place where people don't go because it is dangerous and the
    gods cannot protect them.
17 **shiver** (page 29)
    the way a person's body moves when he or she is either very cold
    or very afraid.
18 **fever** (page 32)
    when your body becomes very hot with an illness, then you have
    a fever.
19 **the world of the Spirits** (page 33)
    some people believe that there is an unseen world all around us.
    Good and bad forces live in this unseen world. These forces are
    the Spirits. Good Spirits help people and bad Spirits are
    dangerous to people. When people die they live another life in
    the world of the Spirits.
20 **medicine man** (page 33)
    a man who knows the secrets of the Spirit world. He can ask the
    Spirits to help people who are sick or in trouble.
21 **explode** (page 41)
    to break into pieces with a loud noise.
22 **commit a crime** (page 41)
    to disobey the laws – in this case, the laws of the gods.
23 **albino** (page 49)
    some people are born with no colour in their skin, hair and eyes.
    This makes these people very white. They have very white skin,
    white hair and reddish-coloured eyes.
24 **missionary** (page 53)
    a person who goes to another country to tell people about their
    God. The missionaries who went from Europe to Africa about
    one hundred years ago wanted the Africans to become Christians.

25 **convert** (page 59)
someone who changes his religion and believes in a new religion.
26 **exclude** – *from the clan* (page 63)
to stop a person joining in the life of a clan. The person is not allowed to do certain things which other people do.

INTERMEDIATE LEVEL

Shane *by Jack Schaefer*
Old Mali and the Boy *by D. R. Sherman*
Bristol Murder *by Philip Prowse*
Tales of Goha *by Leslie Caplan*
The Smuggler *by Piers Plowright*
The Pearl *by John Steinbeck*
Things Fall Apart *by Chinua Achebe*
The Woman Who Disappeared *by Philip Prowse*
The Moon is Down *by John Steinbeck*
A Town Like Alice *by Nevil Shute*
The Queen of Death *by John Milne*
Walkabout *by James Vance Marshall*
Meet Me in Istanbul *by Richard Chisholm*
The Great Gatsby *by F. Scott Fitzgerald*
The Space Invaders *by Geoffrey Matthews*
My Cousin Rachel *by Daphne du Maurier*
I'm the King of the Castle *by Susan Hill*
Dracula *by Bram Stoker*
The Sign of Four *by Sir Arthur Conan Doyle*
The Speckled Band and Other Stories by *Sir Arthur Conan Doyle*
The Eye of the Tiger *by Wilbur Smith*
The Queen of Spades and Other Stories *by Aleksandr Pushkin*
The Diamond Hunters *by Wilbur Smith*
When Rain Clouds Gather *by Bessie Head*
Banker *by Dick Francis*
No Longer at Ease *by Chinua Achebe*
The Franchise Affair *by Josephine Tey*
The Case of the Lonely Lady *by John Milne*

For further information on the full selection of
Readers at all five levels in the series, please refer
to the Macmillan Readers catalogue.

Published by Macmillan Heinemann ELT
Between Towns Road, Oxford OX4 3PP
Macmillan Heinemann ELT is an imprint of
Macmillan Publishers Limited
Companies and representatives throughout the world
Heinemann is a registered trademark of Harcourt Education, used under licence.

ISBN 1–405–07315–2
EAN 978–1–405073–15–8

Things Fall Apart © Chinua Achebe 1958
First published by William Heinemann in 1958 and first published in
Heinemann Educational Books' African Writers Series in 1962

This retold version by John Davey for Macmillan Readers
First published 1974
Text © John Davey 1974, 1992

This edition published 2005

Illustrated by Matilda Harrison
Typography by Adrian Hodgkins
Cover illustration by Matilda Harrison

Printed in Thailand

2009 2008 2007 2006 2005
10 9 8 7 6 5 4 3 2